The Curly-Tailed Advent

Two Very Naughty Piglets

by

Lesley Glover

Illustrations by Kalpart

Strategic Book Publishing and Rights Co.

Book Design/Layout, Illustrations and Book Cover design by Kalpart.

Strategic Book Publishing and Rights Co., LLC
USA | Singapore
www.sbpra.com

For information about special discounts for bulk purchases,
please contact Strategic Book Publishing and Rights Co., LLC. Special Sales, at bookorder@sbpra.net.

ISBN: 978-1-68181-074-4

Table of Contents

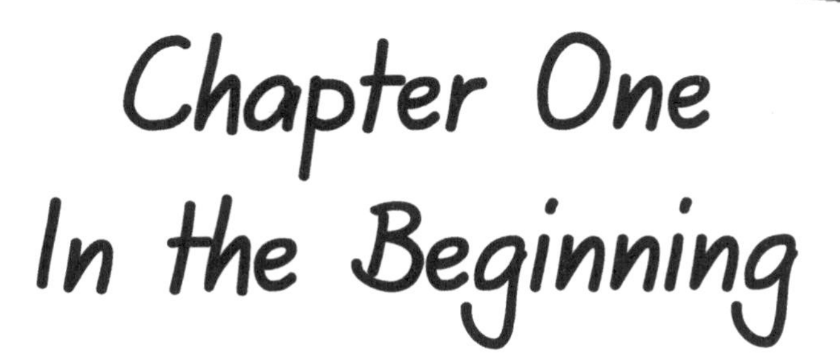

Chapter One
In the Beginning

"Guess what?" Anna the little black dog whispered to her friend Gem.

"I have no idea, and I don't like this silly game you're playing, so tell me," Gem replied in a rather gruff voice, trying to close her eyes and take a little nap, which now seemed impossible because Anna was so busy wagging her tail with excitement that it was causing a draft—which although very pleasant was also irritating for a dog who wanted to go to sleep.

"Well, I just happened to overhear a conversation in the kitchen," Anna sniggered, hardly able to contain herself with the news that was just waiting to burst out like a shaken bottle of pop.

"There are lots of conversations that take place in this house. Which one has got you so excited?" Gem asked in a somewhat reluctant manner, not wanting to appear too enthusiastic to hear the news that Anna was just dying to reveal.

"There's going to be a delivery. New arrivals are coming tomorrow."

"Who's pregnant?" Ellie asked from the sofa, where she too was trying to sleep.

"No, it's not that sort of delivery," Anna giggled and then, desperately wanting to tell all that she'd heard, continued, "This is the sort that comes by car."

"Oh! Parcels, you mean," Ellie said with a grin, knowing quite well that she was making fun of Anna, who seemed more than willing to play along.

"They're not coming by car—they're being towed in a trailer!" Anna snickered. She was really enjoying this game. *I mustn't give it all away too soon*, she thought.

“That means there’s more than one?” Gem piped up.

“Exactly,” Anna snickered again.

“But do you know exactly what they are?” Gem asked, suddenly growing more curious by the minute.

Anna loved being the centre of attention and having a captive audience. She was so excited about what she’d overheard that she wanted to tell them everything all at once, but now that she had a captive audience, she thought she’d string it out a little more, making the tale a little longer. “Well, I did hear something about the fact that they were still young. They had been weaned, though, so they were ready to go.”

“Who and what are ready to go?” Ellie asked as she slid off the sofa to get closer to the action of Anna’s excitement.

Little Anna shared her life with two very large English mastiffs. A beautiful longhaired one called Ellie had a pale silvery grey colour coat that felt as soft as silk. The other one was taller and younger with a short, wiry coat that was a fawn colour with a striking black face, muzzle and ears. She was named Little Gem, although most of the time she was called Gem—or Lettuce by her nan, who thought it rather amusing that such a large dog should be named after a lettuce, which of course she wasn't. In fact, her pedigree name was Little Crystal and her owner, the kind human who looked after all of us so well, thought Gem was easier to say, especially when it came to calling her name out loud while walking through the woods or across the fields. Both mastiffs were kind, gentle and loving souls who adored their little friend Anna. Gem was a year younger than Anna, which meant that they played quite happily together, running after one another playing tag or tug-of-war with some poor toy, while Ellie was quite happy to watch them using up all their surplus energy. Occasionally she'd join in, but nowadays her exercise was more of the passive kind, watching the world go by and taking a leisurely stroll across the fields when the occasion arose.

"Well, I did hear her say piglets," Anna snickered.

"What?!" Ellie squealed. "Piglets! What on earth is she going to do with piglets?"

"Piglets sound like fun," Gem offered, although slightly startled by Ellie's reaction. She thought that maybe Ellie knew something she didn't.

"Piglets," Ellie repeated. "What is she going to do with them? They smell, you know," Ellie said, sticking her nose up in the air.

"I didn't know that," Anna replied, "and I don't know what she's going to do with them. I just know that she's really excited and that they are being delivered tomorrow by trailer and that they are two little girls."

"And where are they going to live?" Ellie asked, butting in with a slightly gruff voice and a frown beginning to form on her face as she tried to make herself look cross, although it didn't work very well. Ellie couldn't look cross even if she wanted to; she just had one of those happy, smiley faces.

"I guess they're going to be living in the far field then," Gem replied with a large smile beginning to appear on her face. "At least now we know why she's been so busy putting up a new fence and building that oversize dog kennel," she laughed as she imagined these two piglets living in the dog kennel—not that she knew what piglets really looked like.

"You mean house," Anna said, sounding relieved. "At least we know it's not for us, so we don't have to worry about being thrown out of the house now."

“Well, I think you should let everyone know what's going on. We can't keep this a secret,” Ellie said with an air of authority, having regained her composure. “Gem, you go and tell the horses and ponies, and Anna, you go and tell the chickens.”

“Right, boss. Anything else, boss?” Anna and Gem both said in unison, running out of the door giggling and whispering to each other. Now that they had been given permission by the top dog, Ellie, they were very eager to tell everyone on the farm the news about the new arrivals that were expected tomorrow.

Chapter Two
New Arrivals

The next morning there was such a strange feeling in the air. Everyone on the farm, from the dogs to the horses and even the chickens, felt a buzz of excitement like electricity; in fact, at first they thought it was probably the local fox prowling around looking for a way into their coop. Whatever it was, it was enough to put them off laying their eggs. "There's definitely something going on today," Gladys said with her usual air of authority. "Has anyone heard anything that would explain this funny feeling I've got?" she asked no one in particular, hoping someone might know.

"Well, I did hear a rumour," Eric the cockerel offered. "It may be nothing, but Anna overheard a conversation in the kitchen, something about new arrivals coming today."

"New arrivals! What new arrivals?" Gladys ruffled her feathers, trying to hide her excitement. "It's the first I've heard of it! Why didn't someone tell me? You know how I like to keep abreast of everything going on," she said as she went to take a swipe at Eric with her wing. He ducked and she missed, and they both ended up laughing. Then Eric, in his usual fine voice, gave a rather loud rendition of his cock-a-doodle-do to broadcast the news that he'd forgotten to pass on the night before. I guess it was one way to relieve the tension that was building as everyone waited in anticipation for these new arrivals to actually arrive.

Anyone would think that Gladys was the boss around here given the way she carried on. Well, I suppose she was in a way, especially when she had her brood of chicks following after her like tiny shadows wherever she went. When armed with her little following, she was definitely a force to be reckoned with, and anyone with any sense gave her a wide berth. As a cat on the prowl, I personally learnt the hard way, and now I stayed well away from her beak, which in the past had aimed itself directly at any convenient soft spot within reach if I so much as dared to look at her babies. As much as I might have been tempted when her chicks were little and a mouthwatering size, it would have been more than my life was worth to have chased after one. I learnt very quickly, as cats normally do, to watch from a safe distance and not to be tempted under any circumstances. When it came to defending her little ones, Gladys was not to be messed with. As for gossip, she just loved to chat to everyone, finding out the juiciest titbits as if she was pulling a worm out of the soft earth—the juicier the better. I had a funny feeling that Eric might have his feathers ruffled a few more times later on for having forgotten to tell Gladys the juiciest bit of news for a long time.

Anyway, as you're already aware, it wasn't a rumour; two little piglets really were on their way to join our happy family down here on the farm. No one knew what they looked like yet, as pigs had never been here before. The news soon got around, as you can imagine; the dogs had told everyone that some new animals were coming but didn't tell them what kind of animal because they wanted it to be a surprise, which only made the buzz of excitement even more intense, with everyone trying to guess what and who the newcomers might be. We all were waiting in great anticipation.

The horses, being big on imagination, were busy making them up to be huge dragons, like the ones they pretended to see in the hedgerows. The dogs didn't seem that perturbed because, of course, they already knew. They just enjoyed making everyone else excited by whispering in their ears. The chickens were a little worried that these newcomers might want to eat them, as it would mean that they wouldn't be able to roam around as freely as they're used to doing. As for us cats, we were interested, but because we were not usually informed of such matters and were never considered worthy of the usual gossip; we had to find these things out in our usual manner—by eavesdropping. We liked to give the impression that we didn't really care, but of course we did. Our air of aloofness helped us to be as nosey and as curious as we liked without being too obvious. Just because the dogs hadn't bothered to tell us didn't stop us from knowing what was going on, as nothing escaped us.

Meanwhile, some miles away, the two new little adventurers were being loaded into a trailer for their first journey, which was about to take them to their new home. They waved good-bye to their mum, brothers and sisters without too much fuss and didn't seem bothered at all. It was as if they knew that piglets had to leave their mum's sty and move on. As they sped along the country lanes, the trailer rocked from side to side, sending them to sleep. As they lay snoozing on the straw bedding, they could feel all the twists and turns in the road as they sped along the lanes, and the bumps caused their little bodies to jump up in the air. But nothing, it appeared, alarmed these two calm, laid-back little piglets.

Suddenly the trailer came to an abrupt stop, which brought them out of their slumber. Their ears pricked up at the sound of dogs barking somewhere close by. It was as if the dogs were letting all the other animals on the farm know of their arrival. They didn't seem to be bothered as they stood in the trailer waiting for the ramp to be lowered; it was as if they'd done this before, only they hadn't—after all, they were still babies. At first, it took a little coaxing to get them to venture out of the trailer and take those first steps onto the ramp, but the rattle of some food in a bucket held under their noses helped, and of course, being piglets, they automatically knew they had to follow it wherever it went. Anything to do with food got their attention, so the bucket led them into a large pen which, as you know, had been made especially for them. This was now their new home.

Great care was being taken to make sure that they didn't escape during the delicate manoeuvre of transferring the piglets from trailer to run, as running around after two piglets in a strange place apparently wasn't on the ticket for today's show, much to the disappointment of all the onlookers, who were hoping for some special and exciting display of humans chasing after these newcomers. Having caught a glimpse of them as they stood on the ramp of the trailer, I thought they would be pretty agile and easily able to outrun the humans, thereby giving us all something to laugh at, but no one obliged. "Oh well, never mind," we all sighed, feeling let down and disappointed. Some of them hadn't even managed to get a good glimpse of these new arrivals. "It's okay for those dogs. They get to see everything," one of the big horses said, and the rest nodded their heads in agreement as they began to depart, walking off the yard and going back to the very important job of eating.

Chapter Three
The Newcomers

All the weeks of preparation had been for these two little newcomers. They had a new wooden house with bright yellow curtains at the window and clean, fresh straw on the floor for their bed. It didn't have a door because pigs like sleeping with lots of fresh air moving around them. In their pen there were lots of weeds and grasses to munch on and plenty of dirt to dig in, as pigs just love rooting around in the dirt. It all looked just perfect to these two new adorable little piglets, whose names were Plumpkin and Penelope, and I have to say, it didn't appear to take them too long to settle in and adjust to their new home and surroundings—and, of course, their new feeding times.

During those first few weeks, they ate and slept a lot, as most babies do. Each time they woke up, they were a little bigger in all ways, longer, taller and heavier. They liked their new names, Plumpkin and Penelope, and as the name suggests, the bigger of the two sisters was called Plumpkin, while the smaller, darker and more spotted one was called Penelope.

I guess this might be a good time to describe these two little piglets. Their hair—well, bristles really—was orange with black spots, which they inherited from their dad, a rather large boar named Clyde whose bristles were really long and dark and whose enormous floppy ears covered his face. He was an Oxford Sandy and Black. (Some people call them plum pudding pigs because they are dark orange with black spots and are a rare breed; in fact, they very nearly died out.) According to his daughters, Clyde was a very nice, quiet, contented chap who was quite happy for the world to pass him by while he slept. The only time he ever appeared to be awake was when it was time to eat. It's amazing what conversations you can overhear when no one knows you're there.

Doris, their mum, was a big black sow with a large white stripe over her shoulders, known as a Saddleback. She had been a very good mum to Plumpkin and Penelope and their eight other brothers and sisters. She had fed them, kept them clean and taught them how to root in the earth for its fine offerings of food. Plumpkin and Penelope inherited characteristics from both their mum and dad, as they had orange hair with black spots. Penelope had more than Plumpkin and was also darker and finer than her sister, but they each had a white flash over their shoulders. At the moment they looked squeaky clean: their white flashes were white, the orange was bright and the black spots looked really black. They were about the size of Anna, a small black Labrador, and they just looked so adorable, unlike Anna who had a tendency to chase us whenever she saw us.

I'm hoping that by now you are a little curious as to who I am and what I look like. Well, I have to say that I'm quite a handsome chap for a cat, with my coat of long, soft white and grey fur. My name is Beau. My brother, Bertie, is a shorthaired tabby cat who is quieter, not so nosey and doesn't quite share my interest in everything that happens down on the farm. I like to think of myself as a smart cat, curious by nature with an eye for detail, a nose for trouble and a purr that would send you to sleep. Our job is to keep the stables and barn clear of mice, and for that we get paid very nicely in cat food. I have to confess that I have actually ventured, very nervously, into the big house on several occasions, but to be honest, Anna is so hot on our tails whenever she sees us that I tend to stay away. I do walk in the garden when I think she's asleep, although a couple of times when she wasn't asleep and her radar eyes spotted me, the very large willow tree that grows in the garden was my lifesaver as I dashed towards it and clambered up its trunk to get out of her way. I think it's just a game to her, but I'm not actually going to put it to the test, as I quite like my long tail. This willow tree with its well-positioned branches allows me to keep an eye on everything without being observed. It is one of my favourite lookout spots because it gives me a good view over the house, garden and paddock, and I can also hear everything that is being said—which, of course, means that I am a font of all knowledge when it comes to gossip.

Now, I have to tell you that during those first few weeks, we had plenty of visitors coming to the farm, all eager to see our new arrivals. Each time someone came, the dogs had to escort the visitors over to their pen, almost as if it was their duty. It also gave them an excuse to bark at the piglets—which, of course, they enjoyed doing; after all, it was their job to bark. It didn't take long for the piglets, Plumpkin and Penelope, to associate the sound of dogs barking with the arrival of food because, as you may have guessed, all these friendly visitors brought them food to eat as a treat, and the piglets wouldn't be so rude as to refuse it. Instead they did what pigs do best: they ate it.

They even had the pleasure of being spoilt by two little girls who visited them regularly. They would go into their pen and sit with them while they ate. They stroked them or brushed their hair, and they even tickled their tummies. So here were these two lovely, colourful piglets attracting all this attention. They had adults laughing and smiling, children cooing and dogs barking, and even cats watching over them like guardian angels.

Then one day some new arrivals, six little miniature Shetland ponies from across the road, came into the field next to their pen, and suddenly their world was transformed.

"Strange creatures," they could hear the ponies whispering to one another.

"What do you suppose they are?" someone asked as they all looked on in amazement.

"We're piglets," Plumpkin called out. "We won't bite you. Don't be scared."

One by one the ponies took turns coming over to the fence to inspect these strange-looking creatures. They had never in their lives seen anything like them. They looked like dogs but weren't, and they smelt different too. It took a lot of courage at first as each took that nervous step forward. Once they made contact through the wire fence that separated them, they were fine, and every day thereafter the ponies would take turns visiting them. The girls enjoyed their company, and because they were only very small ponies, not even as big as their dad, Clyde, it gave them some comfort. Not that they were lonely, for there was so much to do. They had weeds to clear and eat by turning the ground over, checking what was underneath, always looking for any hidden treasure, although I don't really know what they were looking for. They certainly did a thoroughly good job of looking for it. They also had to dig themselves a bathing pool—well, a mud pond really—in preparation for the summer. Pigs just love mud and water, but most importantly they need it when the sun shines, for it stops their skin from drying out; just like humans, they can get sunburnt. We quickly came to realise that where there were pigs, there was always plenty of mud.

Because they had grown so much their pen had to be extended, and it was now much, much longer, which meant they had even more space in which to roam and dig. Now, you would think that this would keep them satisfied and contented, rooting around, digging up the nettles and other weeds that grew there, but unfortunately, after all that digging and turning the soil over, not much grew anymore. However, it would soon become apparent that the outside world was becoming a much more interesting place to be, especially to these two, not so little anymore. Now they were taller, broader and heavier, and they thought that they were big enough to push their way through fences and hedges. And so the fun began.

After many days of planning, they decided that their first escape would be an experiment on how to push their way out under the wire fence. They were not quite big enough to climb over it—yet. I just loved it when I could lie on top of the roof of their house and listen to them while they chatted and made their dastardly plans. It would have been nice to have shared this information, but other than my brother, Bertie, no one seemed interested. I did try. In the end I decided to enjoy their escapades by observing and listening, as I had a funny feeling that with these two, there was never going to be another dull moment. I shall leave you to decide whether I was right or not, as you can now join in on the frolics and antics of these two very naughty curly-tailed piglets.

Chapter Four
A Whole New World

"Plumpkin, are you sure we should be doing this?" asked Penelope, holding back a little, wondering if they should upset the ponies; after all, it was their field. She didn't really want to get into trouble, but she had to follow her big sister, didn't she?

"Of course," Plumpkin replied as she managed to find the piece of fence that moved just enough, allowing her to wriggle her body through. "Easy—come on," she waved, giving words of encouragement for her sister to follow. "See? Nothing to it. Now push harder—there you are, you're through. See, I told you it'd be easy!

Come on, let's go and play with the ponies," she said as she set off running across the field to where the ponies stood, happily grazing, although her excitement fizzled out very quickly when she saw one of them coming towards her.

"Whoa there, Speedy, it's us!" Plumpkin squealed, wondering what to do next as Timmy Twoshoes came trotting towards them. He needed to inspect these newcomers who had trespassed into his field. He was, after all, a stallion and therefore in charge; although he was only thirty inches high, that didn't stop him from thinking he was big. He was a handsome little chap, black and white with odd flashes of brown on his body and in his mane and tail, but of course his presence and character made him feel much, much taller than he really was. It gave him that important air of authority too. These two little piglets couldn't think they could just march into his field without his permission. He'd soon put them right. In the gruffest voice he could find, and puffing himself up with tail and neck arched, he pranced over to them.

"What do you girls think you're doing? You can't just break out of your pen and come into my field." Huffing and puffing, he stood directly in front of them. He wasn't going to let them go any farther. *Pigs indeed in my field. Whatever next?* he thought, standing firmly on all four hooves, trying to prove his point that they should be on the other side of the fence.

"Sorry, Timmy," Penelope squeaked in a shaky, nervous voice. "We thought we'd come out and play."

"Oh, did you?" Timmy replied in his very gruff voice, trying hard to sound serious. He needed them to understand he was the boss. "And what makes you think I want to play with you?" he asked as he looked down his nose at them, trying to make them feel as uncomfortable as he could. "Just because I've spoken to you through the fence doesn't mean I want to play with you!"

"Stop being so grumpy, Timmy," Plumpkin said as she pushed her sister out of the way, walked right up to him and touched him on the nose with her wet snout. She'd had time to think while he'd been moaning, and now she had a plan.

"Don't do that," he said, taking a step backwards. "Don't you know you're not supposed to do that? And don't you know we're not even supposed to like you?" he asked in a voice that was suddenly sounding a little shaky.

"Since when, and what book did you read that in?" Plumpkin asked as she began moving towards him again. She liked this game, and she knew instantly that because he was backing off, she'd won this round. The first one to move away was always the loser.

"Oh, I don't know," Timmy muttered nervously under his breath, moving farther away from them. "Okay, I suppose you can stay, but just you wait. Wait till the human sees you."

Timmy was quite right, of course: horses aren't supposed to like pigs, but, then, that's what humans think. He actually quite liked them—in fact, he was fascinated by them—but he wasn't going to tell them that just yet. He liked to stand and watch them as they played and ran around chasing one another, as little ones do. They always seemed to be getting up to something when they weren't eating or sleeping. *Too much energy, that's what it is*, he thought. "There will be trouble from those two," he muttered as he put his head back down to graze on the nice, tender shoots of green grass.

Timmy shared the field with the other little ponies. Charlie Buttons, a spotted pony, was the oldest pony in the field. He liked to keep his eye on the younger ones, as someone had to keep them in order. He made them mind their manners; one look from him told them when they'd done something wrong. He just liked to remind them now and again of how to behave properly and how to respect their elders. He enjoyed watching the younger ponies play as they ran around the field, kicking their heels up in high spirits as ponies will do. He was like an uncle to his little charges, and now he had taken on two new ones in the shape of spotted, curly-tailed piglets. He didn't mind their being out in the field grazing alongside him, as long as they didn't touch him. As he stood and watched them, he too became a little troubled, as they always seemed to be on the move, never staying in the same place for too long. Just watching them made him feel tired. *Trouble*, he thought. *They're going to be trouble.*

The rest of the little Shetland family was made up of Tiger Tom, the dad, who was a bright, coppery chestnut colour with a long mane and tail, and mum Hettie, a beautiful little pony who looked like a cream-coloured powder puff with a long white mane and tail. Then there was Monty, the baby of the family, who looked just like his dad; his sister, Tilly, who was the same colour as their mum; and finally Auntie Roxy, who was similar in colour to Tiger Tom and Monty, only slightly darker. They all lived together in a herd as one big happy family, enjoying the peace and quiet of living in the country, away from the hustle and bustle of city life.

Monty and Tilly found the piglets great fun to play with, and they soon became very preoccupied, forgetting where they were as they began taking turns chasing one another around the field, until . . .

"What did I tell you? You're in trouble now," Timmy called out, trying to warn them as he saw the human coming. "She's on her way!" he shouted again.

Plumpkin and Penelope were so engrossed in what they were doing that at first they didn't hear Timmy shouting out their names. They so liked this new game that they were playing with Monty and Tilly, even though they couldn't outrun them because they were just too fast, and they could even turn on the spot. *Now, that's clever. I shall have to practice that turn*, Plumpkin thought. All of a sudden she heard someone calling out her name.

"Oops!" squealed Plumpkin. "I think we could be in trouble," she called to her sister as she spied the human marching towards them.

"What do you two think you're doing? Get home *now*!" the human shouted, pointing a finger towards their pen.

So off they trotted like really good little girls, obeying their orders. Actually, they were quite pleased to be going back into their pen, for they were very, very tired after all that playing and running around. You see, having escaped by pushing their way out under the fence, they couldn't get back in because the fence wouldn't move inwards. They hadn't been able to work that bit out, and it wasn't until they were on the other side of the wire fence that they discovered this flaw in their plan, so they knew they were going to get caught. However, it was well worth the telling off because they'd had such a good time playing with everyone.

"You're two very naughty girls. What am I going to do with you?" the human said as she put their dinners down in front of them. They could tell she wasn't really that angry with them because her voice didn't sound cross, and they could tell she was smiling. She was a kind person who always made sure they had plenty to eat, fresh water to drink, and a clean bed of straw to sleep on.

They ate their dinner slowly, enjoying every mouthful as they made all the usual grunting and snorting sounds that piggies make as they eat. It was their way of showing appreciation for the food they were eating, because if there's one thing that pigs love, it's food.

As soon as they had finished their dinner, they curled themselves up in their house on the soft bed of straw and fell asleep, dreaming dreams of ponies and pigs playing together and having fun. Maybe they could play again tomorrow?

Chapter Five
If Only They Had Stayed at Home

Over the past few weeks these two little, or now not-so-little, piglets came to enjoy the thrill of escaping and living amongst the ponies. It was another routine that they'd come to know and enjoy, much like the routine that brought the human to them each morning with their food. Her arrival was always announced by two dogs, sometimes three. Anna, the little black dog, would always arrive first, sticking her nose through the fence to say hello. She liked making contact with the girls, and it was sort of a kiss, much like humans do when they greet one another. Gem might have been bigger than they were, but they weren't afraid of her. To them her size meant nothing, as they had soon discovered that she was all noise as she ran up to the fence barking. They could tell she wanted to be friends but didn't quite know the language they spoke. *In time*, they thought to themselves as they rushed towards the gate, *she'll get the hang of it*. "Breakfast is here!" they squealed.

The wonderful, glorious food was now theirs to eat and was certainly more important than talking to the dogs. "Sorry, guys, we'll talk again later" they snorted as their snouts disappeared into their buckets. This was one routine they excitedly waited for, and nothing would stop them from being there. After their first escape they made sure they could get back into their run, as they didn't want to be caught out again and they couldn't miss a meal, could they? So as far as the human was concerned, they were behaving themselves like the good girls she had asked them to be, staying put in their now extended pen. Their friends the ponies were very good too, as they hadn't told anyone about their daily escapes. Actually, they enjoyed having them around. Quite simply put, they were fun.

It might have stayed that way, and everyone would have been happy. Pigs in bed by teatime tired out from their daily exercise of playing with Tilly and Monty, whose parents were so pleased that their children were occupied and exercised, as it saved their legs from having to chase them around the field when it came to playing tag. Timmy Twoshoes was able to prance around, huffing and puffing as he always did, trying his hardest to look important, letting them all know he was still the boss; he was, after all, the "man of the field." Charlie Buttons and Auntie Roxy looked on in amusement at all the goings-on, appearing not to be bothered either way. However, Charlie found them fascinating and had developed quite a soft spot for them. There was something very appealing about them, and if you were to ask him about them, he'd tell you that they'd grown on him. It certainly wasn't their eyes, which were so small you could hardly see them—not like horses, whose eyes were big and round so they could see all around them. He couldn't quite explain it, and it certainly wasn't their cheekiness that endeared them to him, although they had plenty of it. No, there was definitely something else that appealed to him. Maybe it was because they were always thinking. When they were awake, they always appeared to be on the move doing something, and if they weren't trying to work things out, they were asking questions. They were certainly very busy pigs.

The game of tag normally started when one of the younger ponies decided it was time for a game and got everyone going by running around in a special way, a little like children playing tag in the playground, until the others followed. Then they would try to outrace one another until they all were huffing and puffing, and then they would stop. Sometimes the older ones would just stand and watch the youngsters enjoying themselves, until everyone got tired and decided it was time to rest. Horses and ponies rested a lot; they tended to stand together, sometimes with noses touching tails, especially in the summer, as it helped to keep the flies off their faces. There was always one who acted as a lookout, just in case an intruder came along and disturbed the herd, whilst the others closed their eyes and went to sleep. They didn't need to lie down to sleep, as they could sleep standing up, but as to using their minds as much as these pigs did, *No, we don't do that*, Charlie thought. *Maybe it's because I'm getting a little older and a little slower that these young ones appear to be so quick*, he pondered as his eyes began to close, taking him back to a time when he too frolicked in a field, kicking his heels up and squealing with delight.

"Have you?" Penelope squeaked. The sound of her voice brought him out of his slumber.

"*What?*" he said, sounding cross although he wasn't really—just startled because he'd been far away, running and leaping and eating the greenest, sweetest grass he'd ever tasted. He so wanted to savour the moment, to feel and taste those succulent blades of grass in his mouth. But never mind—something more urgent, in the shape of a pig, needed his attention.

"What?" he repeated. "What now? You're always wanting something. Don't you ever get full up?"

"Didn't you know, pigs don't know when they're full? There's nothing in our brain to register when we've had enough to eat," Plumpkin replied with just a hint of sarcasm in her voice. She stood right behind Charlie so that he couldn't quite see her, but that didn't stop him from knowing she was there. Maybe it was because he could smell her, as pigs definitely wore a different perfume from horses, or even dogs for that matter.

"Might have known you'd have the answer—you normally do. Well, what do you want now?" he asked, looking round as far as he could to see what she was doing.

"Nothing really," she said trotting off. "The moment's gone." And then so was she, with a wiggle of her curly tail. Charlie just stood there in amazement; if he'd had fingers he would have scratched the top of his head. "Unbelievable," he muttered to himself.

"She's a one. Getting too big, they are. They'll find themselves in trouble soon, you mark my words," a small voice said from somewhere behind him.

"Roxy, what did you say?" Charlie asked, blinking as he turned and looked down to where the voice was coming from. It was most unusual for Auntie Roxy to say much, as she was a very quiet pony who was always there in the background, observing and doing her own thing, causing no trouble to anyone. Tilly and Monty always knew that they could run to their Auntie Roxy if they'd been told off, as she always had a kind word for them both and reassuring hugs.

"I said they're getting too big for their trotters, and they'll get themselves into trouble, mark my words," Roxy repeated as she too trotted off, leaving Charlie all by himself.

It was true: they'd been doing just as they liked and the human, who was usually very aware of what the ponies did, had somehow managed not to notice that these two little—or now not-so-little—pigs had been getting up to mischief. Charlie pondered this dilemma for only a moment, as there were other important things for him to do, like getting back to eating or maybe even sleeping. "Well, it's just a matter of time before something happens to spill their cart of rosy red apples," he said aloud to no one in particular.

Actually, it wasn't long before Charlie, Timmy Twoshoes and Auntie Roxy's predictions came true, for everything changed the day a new pony by the name of Tsar came into the field. Tsar was a handsome young chap, much bigger than anyone else in the field. He had come from the New Forest where he'd been born, a large area of open spaces and woodlands in which to roam, when he was just four months old. Like Penelope and Plumpkin, he'd travelled away from his home, his mum and his friends in a trailer that had brought him here to his new home, to live on the farm with the other horses and ponies that lived across the road from the piglets.

He was a young three-year-old gelding, very proud and full of himself, wanting to prove himself as the fittest and the best. Of course, the first one on the scene as this newcomer came into the field was Timmy Twoshoes. He needed to inspect this chap in the same way that he'd inspected Plumpkin and Penelope—and, of course, to tell him that he was the boss.

Well, I guess by now you can begin to imagine what the scene must have looked like as this little pony, who was all of thirty inches high, or 7.2 hands high (that's how they measure horses—four old-fashioned inches equalled the width of a man's hand, or one hand), puffed himself up, arched his neck and tail to make himself look important, then strutted up to this strapping bright bay pony, with a long black mane and tail who was 13.2 hands high, which meant he was fifty inches tall. Well, fortunately for Timmy, on this particular occasion his height was an advantage. Because he was so small, he could nip Tsar on the leg and run away before Tsar had even figured out where to look. Timmy held on to his tail too so that Tsar couldn't get to him no matter how hard he tried. Even his kicks didn't touch Timmy because he was running circles so fast around Tsar that he just couldn't catch him.

Everyone stopped what they were doing and watched this play-fight taking place. This often happened when strange horses were introduced to one another; they had to see who was the strongest and the best, and who was going to be the boss for the day. It seemed like a good opportunity and a chance not to miss, so they all joined in and raced around the field chasing one another, having pretend races. It all ended very happily, with Timmy and Tsar becoming great friends. If they weren't eating close to one another, they were playing together and rearing up. Well, Timmy reared—he stood on his back legs to make himself taller while Tsar got down on his knees, so that they were nearly level and the game was more equal. Even though Tsar had the advantage of age and height, between them there was mutual respect.

All the time that Tsar and Timmy had been playing together, Plumpkin and Penelope had remained hidden in a far corner of the field as if something had told them that this game wasn't for them. They didn't even join in the race afterwards.

"Look at those hooves fly. They look pretty dangerous," they both said aloud as they looked at one another, suddenly realising that this was definitely not the best day for being out of their pen, supposedly enjoying the freedom of the whole field. I wonder if you can guess where they were in the field. Yes, you're right. They were right across the field at perhaps the farthest distance away from their pen, and somehow they had to cross a very large open space to get to safety without upsetting this new pony, Tsar.

While they had been resting and waiting for the game to end, they had been busy hatching a plan whereby they could casually introduce themselves to Tsar when they eventually emerged from their hiding place—which of course they had to, as they couldn't stay there indefinitely. But something went wrong, as they very quickly discovered that Tsar wasn't like the others who'd been curious enough to want to know them. This guy wasn't even going to give them a chance. As soon as he saw them he charged towards them, ears pinned back against his head, neck stretched out and teeth bared. He meant business.

Both gulped at the same time. "Oops, time to get out of here—run!" they both screamed together. "Help!" they squealed and squawked as their little legs ran as fast as they could towards home and safety. Tsar was fast, much faster than they were, and he definitely wasn't the friendly, chatty sort of pony they were used to. He was out to hurt them.

"Help us! Someone save us!" Plumpkin squealed as loud as she could in between breaths, gulping for air as she ran.

"Please, help us!" squealed Penelope, close on her heels and trying her hardest to keep up and follow her big sister. *She'll know what to*

do. She always does, thought Penelope, trusting for once that this time Plumpkin really would know what to do.

Was it instinct? Or was it because Plumpkin had watched Timmy Twoshoes as he played with Tsar? Somehow she had the idea to weave in and out, turning circles around Tsar rather than running in a straight line. It was as if she'd known that if they ran straight for home they would never make it. So far it was working, although she didn't know how much longer they could keep on running. Pigs weren't really designed to run long distances, as their little legs and heavy bodies were meant for other things like digging.

"Keep going," voices shouted from behind them. It was Tilly and Monty coming to their rescue. Of course, they thought it was just another new game for them to play.

"This is great fun. Can we do it again tomorrow?" Monty asked.

Neither of them could reply because they were so puffed out. All they wanted was to get home safely, and it was now in sight with only a few more steps to go—but where was Tsar? Looking round quickly, they could see he'd been stopped by Timmy Twoshoes. Timmy had saved the day; he'd saved their bacon. He was their hero.

After scrabbling back under the fence to safety, they lay there exhausted, their sides heaving as they filled their lungs with much needed air. They were still alive thanks to Timmy. They were home now, back behind the fence and safe from Tsar and his teeth. Within minutes they were fast asleep, and not even the sound of food being rattled around in a bucket could rouse them from their slumbers. Even the sound of the dogs barking heralding the arrival of their dinner didn't wake them. The human looked lovingly over at them asleep on their straw bed and smiled to herself, thinking how peaceful and beautiful they looked. "Just like two little piggy angels asleep in the hay," she said to the dogs, who were sitting by her feet, looking at the two little piglets asleep on the straw. "Such good girls," she whispered softly.

"If only she knew," Anna whispered to Gem, who winked and smiled in reply.

Chapter Six
They Ran All the Way Home

The girls decided to remain in their pen all the time that Tsar was in the field. It wasn't that they were really scared of him; they respected him and understood that, unlike the Shetlands who had been willing to accept them, Tsar wasn't so friendly. They also understood instinctively that it was highly unlikely he would ever be friends with them, and most important, they knew that they were no match for him. To begin with, if they couldn't outrun Monty and Tilly, they certainly wouldn't be able to outrun him, as his legs were much longer than theirs, making him faster in every way. So for their health and safety they decided it was much better for them to remain in their pen. It wasn't as if they didn't have room to root around in. Their pen had been increased yet again and was now over one hundred metres long, so there was plenty of digging they could do—but it didn't quite have quite the same level of thrill factor or excitement as escaping did.

The little ponies, bless them, came up to the fence each day for a chat, and to give credit where credit is due, even Tsar made a huge effort and began to approach them, though not too closely at first because he couldn't quite get used to how different they looked. They had such a peculiar smell about them, which made his nose wrinkle as he puckered his lips and tried to decide what it was. (Horses do this funny thing with their lips when they come across a new smell. They sort of open their mouths and curl up their top lip, as if they are laughing. It makes them look really funny when they do it. I personally use my nose; it's much easier.) Anyway, Tsar persevered and tried his best to get used to the girls—after all, they were neighbours—but something held him back. Even the other ponies tried their hardest to persuade him to like them a little more. They kept telling him that they were good fun to have around and that they wouldn't hurt him, or even try to eat him, because he was much too big for them. There was just something that stopped him from going right up to the fence and saying hello.

Maybe it was because he wasn't with the usual herd of horses that he normally lived with, as they all were still across the road.

The human had put him in the field because she thought that he and Timmy Twoshoes would get on together, and he needed the fun and the exercise. Just as well that it worked out and that they really liked each other, for they played hard, and at times to anyone watching it looked as if they were fighting, but of course they weren't; they were only play-fighting. They respected each other's capabilities and knew just how far they could go without getting hurt. Timmy was a little imp, though. On several occasions we watched him bite Tsar where it hurt most, around the hocks on his back legs, which to you is your ankle. Timmy was teasing him, of course, wanting him to play even more because he never seemed to tire, although the younger Tsar did. He would walk away when he'd had enough, and then they'd stand side by side, eating together like best buddies. It was a fun spectacle and everyone stopped to watch; even the girls were captivated by their playful displays.

Life continued for a while in this safe and comfortable way. The daily routine of the dogs announcing the arrival of breakfast or dinner by barking, telling them it was on the way, gave the girls the signal to sound their own welcome. As they got older they became more vocal, especially when the human brought their food. Encouraged by the dogs, they would grunt, snort and squeal. There was just one problem with all this excitement: they began to forget their manners. I'm sure it was their way of saying, "Good morning. The food is coming, the food is coming," as they excitedly ran up and down their pen, not really knowing what to do first—chase the dogs or catch the human with the bucket. Either way, mealtimes were becoming a little more chaotic. Well, I suppose you could say it was one way of exercising before eating.

Life was good to them, and they had grown even bigger. Summer was now fast approaching, and in preparation for the hot weather to come they had designed and dug out their very own mud bath, larger than the first one, to accommodate their ever increasing waistlines. It was now complete, and each day they would fill it up with water by knocking their water buckets over on purpose so that they could take their bath, albeit a very muddy one. I watched in admiration and smiled to myself on more than one occasion at just how clever these piglets were. They knew exactly what they wanted and how to get it.

Sneakily they had managed to find a new way through the hedge into a sort of no-man's-land, which was to become their secret hideaway because no one could see them behind the thick hedge and brambles. Whilst exploring this new secret place, they had also discovered to their delight another way out, an escape route into the field, which was even more exciting because now they could pop in and out of the field undetected. Even Tsar couldn't see them. Now, as far as they were concerned, remembering of course that these intrepid explorers never saw danger, they thought that it was safe to play with Monty and Tilly again, as they'd really missed their playtimes.

This seemed to satisfy the girls, and on the surface everything looked in order. The human was totally unaware of their daily escapades—and sometimes near mishaps. The ponies continued to be their friends, and even Tsar began getting used to seeing them out and about and was even beginning to accept their presence in the field, as long as they stayed far away from him.

Then one day something happened to upset the applecart of rosy red apples. Can you guess what happened?

It was a beautiful day, and the fancy had taken them to go for a wander, but the one thing they'd forgotten about was how close to teatime it was. Maybe their tummies were a little fuller with all the grass and roots they'd eaten, or maybe the human was early.

So now you have to begin imagining the scene. First, though, I should tell you that pigs aren't the only animals who get excited over food; ponies do too. They get just as excited when they see a bucket. A bucket, any bucket, equates to food in their eyes, and as you know, they're very good at seeing things in the distance, unlike pigs who tend to be a little nearsighted.

So the scene is set. Ponies and pigs were happily eating the grass when the dogs ran into the field. Both knew that the dogs came before the human, who was walking behind carrying a bucket of food for the pigs, whom she thought were safely tucked up in their pen. The ponies were the first ones to move when they spotted the bucket. It was okay for them to run towards her because this was part of the daily game they played. They would check out the bucket just in case it was for them. Don't worry, because later on the ponies would get their own buckets of food, but pig food was different and not for horses—although the dogs quite liked it.

Well, with all this excitement going on, you can imagine what the two little, or now not-so-little, naughty pigs were doing. You're absolutely right. They too were running towards the human, completely forgetting where they were as they began squealing with excitement at the prospect of being fed.

Suddenly there were legs everywhere. Tsar was the first to react, because as you know he still wasn't that sure about the two pigs, although secretly he was coming around to liking them just a little. Tolerating them was one thing, but touching his person was another thing altogether, and here they were running round his legs, going under his tummy. They were much too close for comfort, so he jumped up on all fours, and from the look on his face, he seemed unsure what to do next. I could tell he just wanted to get away from them.

I was watching this fiasco taking place from my favourite perch, the branch of the large willow tree that overhung the garden and field that gave me a really good vantage point from which I could see and hear everything that was going on. I was laughing so much that I very nearly fell off the branch. That certainly would have stopped them all in their tracks, but as I didn't want to stop their fun or mine—or even yours, for that matter—I hung on with my very sharp claws, righted myself, unruffled my fur and then settled myself back down for even more fun to come. I could see in the distance that Tilly and Monty were also finding this so amusing to watch, that they too couldn't stop laughing, and then they just couldn't resist the temptation to join in the fun that everyone appeared to be having. As they ran over to join in the fun, so too did Hettie, Tiger Tom and Auntie Roxy. Timmy of course was there checking out what all the fuss was about, and Charlie just wanted to look in the bucket for any treats that might be there for him. Soon there were so many legs and feet all going round in circles that it made me feel dizzy just trying to keep up with who was where and who was chasing who. Then the dogs decided to join in too, as they couldn't possibly miss out on this opportunity to chase after the pigs. Well, I suppose this was the first time they'd seen them outside their pen.

At this stage of the proceedings, I began to feel really sorry for the poor human, who was just standing there, unable to move. From what I could see, I don't think she knew where to look or what to do. The pigs were still running around in circles. I think they were really enjoying themselves on this roundabout of fun, except they kept getting in the way of the ponies, who, because they were used to them, were now beginning to enjoy this game too—except for Tsar, who was

going around in circles trying to get away from them. Fortunately, like all the games the ponies play, they quickly ran out of steam, and this merry-go-round of fun soon slowed down without anyone getting hurt. As we all—that is, except for the human—know, the ponies, including Tsar, were used to them because of their daily exploits.

It was the best laugh I'd had in ages, and I have to give it to those girls—they certainly knew how to dance a fair jig. Everyone returned to what they had being doing beforehand: eating, except for Penelope and Plumpkin, who were now waiting patiently by the gate of their pen for the food to arrive. They stood there so calmly, as if butter wouldn't melt in their mouths, only the poor human wasn't as calm when she arrived with the bucket that had caused so much fun. As she opened the gate to let them into their pen, she pointed her finger to indicate where she wanted them to go. "In!" she ordered them.

"I think she's cross with us," whispered Penelope as they both walked in very quietly and went to where she'd placed their food. Try as they might, they couldn't be polite; they just had to tuck in. Food, after all, was food, and they weren't even out of breath.

Well, I guess you can imagine what happened next. The fence was checked and double-checked, with every little hole filled in. Every likely escape route was located and boarded up with more string, more nails, more wood and more wire. The human was determined not to let them escape again. She just didn't know these determined pigs very well. A fence to them was just a challenge, not something that was meant to keep them in.

"Ahh, oh well!" they sighed contentedly to themselves, remembering what fun they'd had, with everyone, even the dogs, chasing one another. It had been a perfect day.

"There's always tomorrow, and she hasn't found our secret," smiled Plumpkin just before she closed her eyes and went to sleep. A big sigh followed from Penelope as she too closed her eyes and went to sleep. As large smiles spread across their faces, I wondered if they were both beginning to dream, remembering what fun they'd had, or maybe planning for tomorrow.

Chapter Seven
The Mission

The day arrived when it was time for Timmy Twoshoes to leave the field he called his own. He went off in a trailer, similar to the one that Penelope and Plumpkin had arrived in. Apparently, Timmy Twoshoes had only been staying with the other ponies as a lodger while his owner found him a new home.

“Fancy that,” Penelope said to Plumpkin. “The way he carried on about his field, acting as if he owned it, inspecting everyone who came into it. Who'd have thought it?”

“He was a nice little chap, and I'm sure he really

liked us. He played with us as if we were his friends; and he did save us," replied Plumpkin, taking in a gulp of air, almost as if she was trying to stop herself from getting emotional over Timmy's departure. "I'm really going to miss him" she said as she turned away.

The Shetland family and the piglets all stood together and watched as Timmy was led out of the field and up the ramp of the trailer. They waved their good-byes, but there was no response from Timmy because he was already too busy inspecting the trailer. "Oh well, let's hope he has someone to boss around in his new home," Plumpkin said as she watched the car and trailer move off, taking Timmy Twoshoes towards his new home.

Soon after Timmy's departure, the ponies left them as well, going back across the road to live with the big horses. It was just far enough away for them not to be able to see their friends anymore, and being left by themselves meant that their lives weren't quite the same without the daily visits and playtimes with their pony friends. Tsar never did manage to feel that friendly towards them, so they didn't miss him at all.

Both I and my brother, Bertie, had taken a very keen interest in watching these two new arrivals on the farm. Cats are curious creatures by nature, but something about these newcomers told us that if we watched them closely enough, we would be in for some very special treats, which up to now had proved to be the case. I did feel a little sorry for them now that their friends had left them, and although I tried to make myself known to them, I think I may just have been a little too small for them to have noticed my presence. So instead I decided then and there that I would follow them wherever they went; I would be the fly on the wall, so to speak, so that I could be as close to the action as possible. I thought that the naughtiest one, Plumpkin, wouldn't be able to contain herself. It just wasn't in her nature to be good, and I'll leave you to be the judge of whether I was right or wrong.

Meanwhile, the girls were a little despondent, as there wasn't that much fun in escaping anymore because they didn't have anyone to play with. They began to yearn for some new adventures and excitement to pass the day. It wasn't that they were really unhappy; it was just that something was missing in their lives. It wasn't as if they didn't have enough food to eat. They had two meals a day of tasty pig nuts, and then there were always some extra tasty treats too, like bananas, apples, avocados, pineapple, nectarines, cherries or strawberries, and occasionally some dog food. They didn't really like celery, peppers or even onions, and they didn't think much of oranges either. They never left anything in their trough; they ate every single morsel of food they liked. Life for them should have been really good, and I suppose it was, unless you were adventurers seeking excitement. And that's just what these two little, or now not-so-little, naughty piglets were seeking—only no one except them and me knew it.

Plumpkin, as you've probably already guessed, was the leader, so when she decided it was time to find a new adventure, that meant it was definitely the right time to begin making new plans. According to her, they needed something to do. They weren't even put off by the fact that the human now made daily checks on the state of the fencing, looking for any holes that might have appeared overnight. Apparently she was worried they would escape again, as they might be tempted to go wandering. Now that was a thought!

Plumpkin, the fidgety one, was always on the go, thinking, planning or talking. She had so much to say, and she even grunted in her sleep. Penelope was getting used to these mini adventures and was always happy to go along with her sister, although if she'd been given a choice, she would have happily stayed in the pen and slept all day and night—waking up, of course, when the food arrived, as it did twice a day.

Sometimes, when visitors came to see them, more food would come too. It wasn't hard for them to associate humans with food because, as far as they were concerned, the two always went together. So whenever they saw another human coming towards them, they would squeal with delight, getting themselves excited at the prospect of being fed again.

To make life a little more exciting, and with a challenge or two thrown in for good measure, they both decided to keep the secret opening as a last resort in case of emergency. They needed to stretch themselves—you know, work things out, like how to get over or under the fences. You may have gathered by now that there was more to Plumpkin's plan; it wasn't just about getting out of the pen and into the field. There was a bigger goal to aim for: the garden and the dogs. All she could see that separated them from her goal was another fence, and as you know, Plumpkin didn't view fences as problems, only challenges to work around. She really wanted to find the dogs that came to their pen each day. There was always such a lot said between them, more noise than anything else, as both parties always got excited about the arrival of the food. She thought and hoped that they could be friends as they were with Monty and Tilly. She really did miss playing their game of tag. *Perhaps*, she thought, *the dogs might like to play tag too.* It might have been a good plan at this point to have asked the dogs if they wanted to be friends, but to be honest, she didn't quite know how because they didn't speak the same language. I guess that would have been a bit too simple and easy for Plumpkin, who would then have been left without a challenge.

Anna, Little Gem and sometimes Ellie, the big hairy one, didn't really think too much of the pigs. They liked running into the field, heralding the arrival of the pigs' breakfast and dinner, but, then, dogs liked running around anyway. Ellie thought when they first arrived that they would make a good dinner, but as they grew bigger she wasn't too sure. Her legs didn't work quite as fast as they used to. Little Gem wasn't too sure as to whether or not she should be friends with them. Something told her she should be running after them, not talking to them. Anna, on the other hand, liked them, having touched noses and snouts with them through the fence on several occasions, so she thought that they might be good to play with. Part of their daily ritual was to run alongside the pigs as they ran up and down their pen, waiting excitedly for the human to arrive with their breakfast. At least with the fence separating them, the dogs felt that they had the upper hand; that is, they thought they were the ones in charge.

Even though the dogs barked at the pigs, they knew they didn't mean them any harm because their tails were always wagging; it was just their way of talking. These two pigs, now not so little, were afraid of nothing—not that they'd been exposed to lots of scary things shut away in a large pen in a field, away from most things. But then, how do you know you're scared of something until you meet it? You don't. These two certainly didn't, so as far as they were concerned, they were the bravest and most adventurous pigs in the world—that is, of course, the world they knew.

Success came quite quickly, as Plumpkin found a new way out of their pen. Having checked the fence many times over, she eventually found a small section of the wire fence just loose enough for her to wriggle her snout through, and then her head, and then her body until she was standing in the field looking through the fence at Penelope.

"Whoopee! Freedom! Come on!" she squealed with joy, running round and round in circles with excitement, urging her sister to follow as quickly as possible. "The first thing we'll do is wander around the field, gradually making our way over to the fence that surrounds the garden. Then we'll check it out for possibilities," ordered Plumpkin, sergeant major of surveillance unit number one.

"Yes, sir," replied Penelope. "At the ready, sir, after you," she said, standing at attention and even trying to salute, although it was a little difficult because she couldn't quite get her front trotter up as her large, floppy ear got in the way.

Off they set at a trot, their snouts pointing towards their goal as if Plumpkin had any intention of wandering around the field. They were on an important mission; their goal was in sight, and with no Tsar to stop them and no ponies to distract them, they were onto a winner.

"Target approaching," whispered Penelope, looking about her. "All clear, sir. No sign of anyone. No dogs, no human."

Plumpkin had learnt something from her past mishaps, and that was not to be too hasty. As no one was about, she could now take her time to check everything out. At first she was a little disappointed to find no one at home, because she'd been seeking excitement and had so wanted the dogs to be there. The real mission, as far as she was concerned, was to play with them. What she hadn't quite figured out yet was whether the dogs would want to play with them.

The fence surrounding the garden was easy and offered no real challenge, as there were so many places they could get through. They could crawl under rails or jump through them, and there was even an open garden gate they could walk through. Obviously the human wasn't expecting them. "Well," Plumpkin said, "just for today we won't stay, as no one is at home."

And with that, they both turned around and trotted off, happy to go back into their pen via their secret entrance and wait like good girls until their dinner arrived. It had been a successful mission, a reconnaissance to check everything out so that their next visit would be successful. After all, there was always tomorrow.

Chapter Eight
The Garden and the Dogs

Well, would you believe that after all their planning on how to escape, the human did something so unexpected that it left these two little—or now not-so-little—pigs totally dumbfounded? The human deliberately left the gate to their pen open. She actually wanted them out. Can you believe it?

"Do you think it's a trap?" Penelope asked her big sister "Or can we really run free?"

"Well, there's only one way to find out, but let's finish our breakfast first and then we'll investigate," muttered

Plumpkin, who was too busy eating her breakfast to be distracted, even if it meant freedom.

Of course, there was no real exploring to do because they'd already done it all during their previous adventures. The field had been thoroughly checked out—so had the fence and so had the garden—so all they had to do now was play.

I watched them from my usual perch wolfing down their breakfast in such a hurry that I had a feeling they would definitely be getting up to some form of mischief today; after all, you cannot stop two naughty piglets from being naughty. I decided it was all in their curly tails. As soon as they finished their food, they were off dashing across the field as if they were late for an appointment.

"Hang on a minute. What's she doing?" Plumpkin squealed as they both skidded to a halt, just before crashing into the fence, because the human was bending over mending it. "Has she read our minds?" Plumpkin asked as she looked at her sister, screwing her face up as if she was trying to determine whether or not she had scuppered her plan. "Did you tell someone that we thought the garden fence was an easy challenge? Did they say something to the dogs?" Plumpkin asked outright.

"No! I never said a word to anyone," Penelope replied with a smile, as she had spotted something Plumpkin had missed. "Anyway, she's not mending the fence—she's putting in more rails so we can still play." They both tittered and laughed because they knew what was coming next; as you know, they were on a mission, and the opportunity to show the human what they could do was now one that they couldn't possibly miss. So without any hesitation on their part, they found just the right spot—one, of course, that the human hadn't yet found—and they were through. They didn't even need to crawl under a rail because jumping over one was much easier. Success followed them so easily with hardly any effort at all; now that they were through, they were exactly where they wanted to be: in the garden.

"Hang on!" shouted the human. "I thought you'd be happy in the field, running around in all that space. Get out of my garden!" she shouted as she ran after them. But it was too late—by the time she reached them, they'd found what they were looking for: the dogs.

Ellie, the big hairy mastiff, was fast asleep on the patio. Although quite large in size, she was a very gentle dog who liked nothing better than to lie outside and watch the world go by. She'd bury herself beneath the hedges and small shrubs that grew in the garden, and sometimes, just to make herself even more comfortable, she'd dig herself a hole to lie in. She had the most beautiful silvery grey coat that was long, soft and silky. Because she was such a big dog, there was plenty of hair to keep her warm.

She just loved travelling in the car with her head out the window; fast or slow, her head was there for all to see, and she certainly was a sight to behold. She made everyone smile when they saw her happy face smiling back at them, complete with floppy ears. When the piglets first arrived, she ran after the trailer baying like a hound, following the scent of something really interesting. As they grew, though, she wasn't too sure, and then when she saw them running around the field with the ponies, she knew they were far too big for her to hunt and hoped they would never get into the garden. If they did, she wouldn't know what to do. She had already decided that if that happened, the best thing she could do was to lie low, keep quiet, bury her head and hope that they would go away and leave her alone.

Of course, as she lay fast asleep on the patio dreaming dreams, as dogs do, of chasing rabbits and little things, she was completely unaware of what was going on—until Plumpkin decided to touch noses. Ellie awoke with such a start that she didn't know where to look or what to do. Thinking it was best if she stayed perfectly still, even holding her breath, she tried to ignore this big pig that was looking directly at her; in fact, she was so close that Ellie could see her little eyes, which were normally hidden under those huge floppy ears. She tried her hardest to become invisible to this intruder in her garden. *What happened to the little piglet that I wanted to eat when she first arrived?* Ellie thought. *When did she get so big? She's enormous; she didn't look this big behind the fence or even in the field.* "Help!" she cried out. "Help me, someone! Save me, please!"

Help soon arrived in the shape of another pig, as Penelope just wanted to say hello too, although this wasn't the sort of help that Ellie had been praying for. She knew she could just about cope with one pig, but now that this other spotty creature had turned up and was sniffing her too, she was off. Standing up, Ellie did what any dog would do: she barked.

"Hey, you two, respect please for an elderly person," she barked at them. "Don't you know it's rude to poke and prod someone when they're asleep?"

"Sorry," they replied in unison. "We only want to play."

“Well, don’t be so rough. We’re only dogs, you know,” Ellie replied, beginning to walk away in the hope of finding a safer, quieter place to be—only she didn’t quite get there because, at the sound of Ellie barking, Gem ran over to see what all the noise and fuss were about. With Gem on the scene, Ellie quickly found her courage and the two of them began to chase the piglets, who, thinking this was a new game, began to chase the dogs. So they all were going round and round in circles, chasing one another’s tails.

“This is fun!” I heard Plumpkin shout to Penelope. “This is the best game ever.”

“It’s great, isn’t it? Let’s hope they don’t get tired too soon,” Penelope laughed.

The human could only look on in amazement. Anna, who was a small dog in comparison to Ellie and Little Gem, thought that sixteen legs were probably enough to be running around one another, so she played it safe and stayed by the human’s side, trying her hardest not to laugh at the spectacle that was taking place before her.

“This is such a great game!” shouted Penelope to Plumpkin as they continued to run around in circles.

"I don't think so," panted Ellie, who wanted to get off this strange roundabout game she was playing against her wishes. *Oh, for a quiet life*, she thought. "Someone please stop them before I faint," she called out, hoping the human might hear her plea.

Help came not a minute too soon from the human, as if she'd heard Ellie's plea after all. She spoke very sternly to all of them. "That's enough. Stop now. Get off them!" she shouted, trying to stop those two naughty pigs from chasing her beloved dogs. She could see that Ellie had had enough and somehow managed to get her safely into the house.

"Oh well! Guess that game's over," the piglets mumbled to themselves as they moved away, looking for something else to do. Within no time at all they were on to their next game, rooting up the patio paving stones, which definitely looked more fun.

"There must be lots of grubs and roots under these slabs," Plumpkin said, licking her lips as her nose disappeared into the wet, soft earth beneath the paving slab she'd just managed to overturn.

"Lovely grub," echoed Penelope, whose snout was also sifting through the damp soil as she looked for her next snack.

The human, having sorted the dogs out, now stood there feeling quite helpless as to what to do next. Overhead, dark clouds were forming, and somewhere in the distance she could make out the sound of thunder rumbling, warning that a storm was approaching.

"I guess this wasn't the best day to let you two out," she spoke to them, trying to get their attention, as they continued to sniff their way around her garden, completely oblivious to her. As usual, they didn't stay too long in any one area, for there was just too much to see and do. The last time they'd been in the garden, they'd been such good girls that they hadn't stayed to investigate because no one was at home. Today, though, they were having so much fun.

"What am I going to do with you two now?" she asked, looking for some inspiration, help or support from either Little Gem or Anna, who were watching at a safe distance from the other side of the garden, while Ellie stood safely watching the proceedings from behind the kitchen door. Running alongside the pigs while they were in their pen was one thing, but facing them in her garden was another. She might have been taller than they were at the moment, but they were all muscle and had large snouts with lots of teeth. As far as she was concerned, there was no contest; they were the winners.

Unbeknown to the human, she hadn't quite secured the back door to the kitchen when she put Ellie inside, and out of the corner of her eye, Plumpkin could just make out a reflection in the glass—which of course she just *had* to go and investigate. Looking at the door, she thought she saw something familiar, and to her surprise, when she tried to talk to the other pig, not knowing that it was herself, the door moved. It opened into a room full of smells—wonderful, delicious food smells. "Quick, Penelope, come and see what I've found!" she shouted to her sister excitedly.

"Where has the human gone?" Penelope asked, trying to speak through a mouthful of soft earth.

"Don't know. You've got to come and see this," Plumpkin called out to her sister again. "This is *so* exciting. Quick, before she sees us. Come on."

Well, you can imagine their delight at finding themselves in the kitchen. Ellie certainly wasn't going to stop them. She'd already made up her mind that she was better off somewhere else and had made her escape into the back of the house, where hopefully they wouldn't find her.

"What's this?" asked Penelope upon finding a bowl full of water. "Oops! That didn't last long," she said as the bowl of water went all over the carpet. "Ah! This looks more hopeful," she mumbled, this time with a mouthful of dog biscuit.

"What have you found?" asked Plumpkin, trying to get her head inside the biscuit barrel at the same time as her sister. "Ummm! That's tasty," she said as she kicked the barrel over. Now there was dog biscuit being mixed in with the spilt water, all going into and over the nice carpet on the floor. Not that they were bothered by the mess—they had more important things on their minds, like the human who was now approaching, running towards them with a look of horror on her face.

"What have you two done?" she asked in a rather stern voice, looking as angry as she could whilst at the same time trying to hide the laughter she felt rising in her throat as she looked at the mess in her kitchen. It really was quite a sight, but there was no use in crying over spilt water and dog biscuit. Not quite knowing what to do next, she needed time to think. She needed a plan and fast, but first she needed to get the piglets out of her kitchen.

"Out! Get out *now*!" she shouted at them, pointing her finger in the direction she wanted them to go, out the back door. Of course, being the good girls they were, they happily obliged. *If I could get a rope around them, like a harness, I could maybe lead them back into the field and into their pen*, she thought. Although at this stage she didn't even know if they would walk nicely with her like the dogs did when they went for a walk. She knew that they normally responded and did anything for food, but because they'd already eaten so much, she wasn't sure if they would follow her like normal. Besides, the food was too far away and she needed to get them out of her kitchen and garden right now.

Armed with some rope and with Anna by her side to help, she eventually managed to get them into a position where she thought she could catch one of them. Well, it was her first day at this new game, so Penelope obliged by allowing herself to be caught; well, that is, she allowed the rope to be put around her neck and then she ran, encouraged of course by her sister, who thought this was a brilliant new game. Was it a human chasing a pig with a rope, or was it a human being pulled along by a runaway pig? She wasn't sure, but it was so funny to watch that her sides were aching from laughing as she watched her sister running around the garden with the human flying behind her.

"Yippee!" squealed Penelope in delight as she ran across the garden, pulling behind her the human, whose legs and arms were flapping around all over the place. She had no control whatsoever over what Penelope was doing or where she was going; all she could do was follow. Ellie and Gem, who had been keeping themselves away at a safe distance, decided that it looked like fun and joined in by following—or were they chasing? This, of course, encouraged Penelope to run even faster, and all round the garden they went—in, out and even over the flower beds and round the trees—until, exhausted, the human had to let go of the rope she'd managed to get onto Penelope, who, now that she was free, ran over to join her sister. This meant that the two piglets could now play with the two dogs.

"Oh! We forgot to tell you that we're quite fit piglets. Every day we exercise by running across the fields," laughed Penelope as she looked back to see the human looking totally bewildered with a bright red face, holding her sides and gasping for air.

"What am I to do now?" she asked out loud, in the hope that some bolt of inspiration might strike her as the sounds of rolling thunder grew closer and the clouds got even blacker. "There's nothing else for

it," she said, replying to her own question. As you and I both know, that of course meant food.

She hoped that by placing a bucket of food under their noses and rattling the nuts to attract their attention, they would begin to walk after her even though they were probably full from all the food they'd already eaten since getting into the garden. Naturally, of course, being such good and obedient girls, they followed her as requested, and she led them out of the garden, across the field and safely back inside their pen.

"Why didn't she ask us to go home?" asked Plumpkin, winking and smiling at Penelope.

"We would follow her anywhere for such a lovely reward," Penelope laughed, licking her lips at the thought of those extra rations.

Just as they got back inside their pen and the human gave them their reward of food, the heavens opened and the rain came pouring down. As soon as they had finished eating, they both ran to their mud bath and dived in. "Ah! That feels *so* good. A perfect end to a perfect day," grunted Plumpkin.

“I second that,” squealed Penelope with delight as she lay in the muddy water, enjoying every moment.

They were such good girls. Every day they had a bath, the muddier the better. They couldn’t help but laugh as they watched the human run back across the field, already soaking wet from the rain. “Well, I guess that’s one way of cooling down,” Plumpkin snickered. “Personally, I prefer our bath. It’s better for our skin.” And with that, they both closed their eyes and went to sleep, perhaps revisiting the kitchen and all its wonderful smells.

Chapter Nine
Oh No! Not the Kitchen Again!

Bertie and I had managed to find many convenient places to hide ourselves so that we could observe all the carryings-on of these naughty, but very nice and very comical, piglets. With such a good view of all their antics, I have to say that at times our sides ached from having laughed so much. I even lay on the roof of their sty so that I could listen to their chatter, and even then on many occasions I thought I'd given myself away because I couldn't stop myself from laughing at Plumpkin's audacious plans.

I'm wondering where to begin now, because it would appear that these two little—well, now not-so-little—pigs seemed to think they could do anything they liked and go anywhere they wanted. Could nothing stop them? Well, it would seem that the fences and hedges were now just targets for Plumpkin and Penelope to conquer. However, the main attraction to them was the fence around the beautiful garden, which was like a huge magnet drawing them towards it so that, every time they were out, they had to inspect it to see if they could find a new way through it or over it. The human had managed to stop them from going under it by putting in an extra rail all the way round, but no matter how much room they had in their field, it seemed it just wasn't enough. They needed the adventure and excitement of being naughty, and the place for that was on the other side of the fence.

It amused them to watch as the human got to work on the fence again and again. Hammer, nails and more rails came out to fill in the gaps, and the fence definitely began to take on an artistic patchwork effect—which was fine if you were into that sort of thing. However, to these two naughty pigs it wasn't even making it more difficult for them to gain access to the treasured garden, which was their goal, because no matter how hard she tried, the human couldn't quite work out how or where they were getting through. Her biggest problem was that she hadn't quite caught on to how amazingly intelligent these pigs were, and, bless her, she kept thinking that they would stay in their field and be the good girls she so wanted them to be. In her own way, she wanted what was best for them, which she thought was room to roam in a field full of tasty grass to eat and toys to play with. They, on the other hand, sought only three things: the company and fun of the dogs, the human, and the food they associated with her.

"Well, what do you think?" Penelope asked Plumpkin. "Do you think she's mended the fence well enough that we won't be able to get through it?"

"No, I don't think she's that clever. There'll still be enough places for us to get through. Come on!" squealed Plumpkin. "Let's go and play!"

"Yippee!" they both squealed in excitement at the prospect of yet another adventure. Yesterday had been such fun, and even though the human thought she'd fixed the fence, they knew she still hadn't spotted their secret opening, hidden from view; that was there just in case they needed it.

"It's a bit quiet. Where are the dogs?" Penelope asked, looking around just in case she might spot some movement in the garden.

"Guess they've gone out," replied Plumpkin. "It's not so much fun without them, so let's take a nap and wait for their return."

"Good idea," Penelope replied. She could always sleep anytime, anywhere. They soon settled down and went to sleep—dreaming, I guess, of the fun to come.

The human, unaware of their mighty plans, had gone off shopping with the dogs, feeling very confident that her handiwork would contain the pigs. The dogs always accompanied the human on her shopping trips because they enjoyed riding in the car. Ellie took great pleasure in sticking her head out the car window, making people smile as they drove by, which they did when they saw her big, hairy head and floppy pink tongue hanging out the window and her ears flapping in the wind.

Even though those naughty pigs appeared to be fast asleep, as soon as they heard the car turn into the driveway they were awake, ears pricked to the sounds of the dogs and the human. This was the moment they'd been waiting for; now their fun could begin.

The first thing the human did was to go out into the garden to see where the pigs were. Of course, you know these pigs so well by now that I'm sure you already know what they did next.

You're absolutely right: the two pigs ran at full speed towards the fence, having already picked out the best place to jump through. For some reason, maybe luck or just bad timing, the human was standing right in front of their appointed spot. As she stood looking at it, her hand went to her mouth as she suddenly saw the gap she'd left them, and before her very eyes—before she could do anything to stop them—they leapt through the rails and were off, across the garden as fast as their sturdy little legs could carry them. Their chosen target of the day, of course, was the kitchen, and nothing stood between them and their goal. What luck—the door was open again, just waiting for them to enter into the kitchen, and there were no dogs to stop them either, as they were somewhere else inside the house. Maybe something had warned them that those two naughty pigs were on the loose looking for fun.

"Whoops! What happened to the carpet?" squealed Plumpkin as she skidded across the floor, hitting the water bowl and spilling water everywhere—again. They were in piggy heaven with all the delicious smells of food wafting into their nostrils; and today they'd hit the jackpot: the human had left her shopping bags on the kitchen floor, just waiting for their snouts to explore them and find some really tasty morsels of food inside. Yummy!

"What's this? Food! Oh goody!" Penelope squealed as she spotted the line of shopping bags.

"Where?" Plumpkin squealed, slipping and skidding sideways on the wet floor, trying her hardest to get her four trotters to work together.

"Behind you, look behind you! Oops! Here comes trouble. Quick, let's go," squealed Penelope. "The human is here. Quick, grab something and run."

Well, as much as she would have loved to stop and rummage through the bags, Plumpkin knew that she had to be quick, so she picked up the first thing she could get her mouth around: a roll of dog food. Yummy!

Suddenly a voice roared at them, "What do you two think you're doing? Get out, *now*!" the human shouted. The piglets tried their hardest to turn and run, but their trotters kept slipping and sliding on the wet floor, and as their feet slipped their bodies did too. They crashed into each other in their haste to get out. There was also another slight problem—or should I say three slight problems?—that prevented them from obeying her orders: the three dogs. Having heard all the noise, they'd come into the kitchen to see what was going on. In fact, they'd

been quietly observing the pigs trying to walk on a wet floor, finding it so amusing to watch that they'd kept themselves hidden in the shadows, but now that the human was here, they too could join in the fun.

Suddenly the kitchen appeared to be quite crowded with two pigs, three dogs and one human. Everyone except the human was attempting to get out. For several moments in the chaos that followed, there were lots of legs going in different directions as the pigs ran round in circles, apparently being chased by the dogs, who thought that this was great fun, especially because they felt they had to make it look as if they were being really useful in their attempt to get the pigs out of the kitchen. The pigs really needed to escape the human and the dogs to hang on to their prizes of snatched goodies, but for them the major problem was that there were just too many legs all trying to move in the same direction, and the wet floor seemed to be getting more and more slippery. All the while that this fiasco was going on, the human just stood there unable to move, her hands on her hips and her face like thunder watching, yet underneath you could tell that she was desperately trying not to laugh at the spectacle unfolding in front of her. Legs and trotters began to get tangled, and the more the piglets tried to escape, the more they slipped and slid over the wet tile floor as if it was a skating rink.

Fortunately for all involved, the doorway became visible enough for the two pigs to make a run for it with their prizes still held firmly in their mouths. Plumpkin had her roll of dog food and Penelope had a packet of tomatoes (which was all she could snatch). Well, it was better than nothing.

"Whoopee!" came the sound of delight from two very naughty pigs who would have quite happily gone back for more, but the human had other ideas.

"Home!" commanded the stern voice from behind them. "Get home now," it boomed again. They both looked round to see the hand going up with the finger pointing in the direction of you know where.

Reluctantly they obeyed, knowing that their fun for the day was over as they made their way back towards their pen. Penelope looked round to see the human following them, and to her surprise and delight she saw that she was carrying a bucket. *More food!* thought Penelope. *Maybe it's not such a bad day after all.*

"Quick," she whispered to Plumpkin. "More food's coming. Be good and run home."

“Okay,” replied Plumpkin, her mouth already watering at the thought of more food as she ran ahead, wagging her curly tail with delight.

“This has been a very grand day today,” she muttered to her sister in between mouthfuls of bananas and melon. “What a lunch we’ve had, a feast on top of tomatoes and dog food. Do you think we’ll get lunch tomorrow too?” Penelope asked; hoping of course that they would.

Well, I suppose you can probably guess what the human did next. You’re absolutely right in your thinking. More fencing went up with more string and more nails. The dogs stood dutifully by her, watching as each new piece of fence went into place.

“Serves them right,” Anna said to Gem. “Who do they think they are, eating our food?”

“I know,” replied Gem, “and the cheek of them invading our home too. It’s about time she put a stop to them coming into our garden.”

“Do you think that fence will keep them out?” asked Anna, “It looks a bit higgledy-piggledy, you know—a bit of this and a bit of that. Will it be strong enough?”

"I don't know," Gem replied. "I suppose it looks artistic, if you're into that sort of thing; but I do know one thing for sure—we can't get into the field now to chase the rabbits."

"They've taken away our fun," Anna said as she sulked off, thinking of all those rabbits she couldn't chase.

There were many occasions when we could have told the dogs about their plans to escape—forewarned them, so to speak—but we thought it best not to. Well, my brother, Bertie, liked to think it was one way of getting back at the dogs for chasing him. The little black one, Anna, never gave him any peace. Whenever she saw him—and boy did she have good eyesight—she gave chase and barked after him as he made his escape. He said she was always making him jump out of his skin, so we decided not to spoil anyone's fun, especially our own and of course yours, as you are now joining in on their adventures.

I have to tell you that once those two very naughty pigs had eaten their lunch and settled down for an afternoon nap, nothing disturbed them, not even the sound of the hammer knocking more nails into the fence in the hope of keeping them out of the garden. Well, I guess there was always tomorrow.

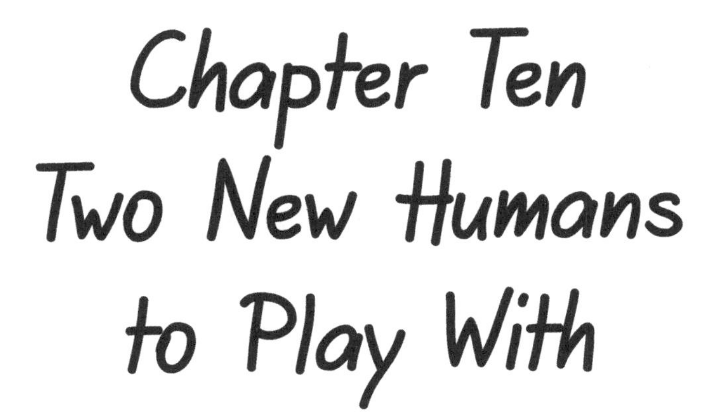

Chapter Ten
Two New Humans to Play With

Well, you're probably wondering whether the human was successful in keeping those two now not-so-little pigs in their field. The answer was yes, for a little while at least, and the reason was that she was off on her holidays, so the fences had to be secure. Now, whether Plumpkin and Penelope knew this and had decided to be good for a few days, I'll leave you to decide.

Although there were two new humans looking after

all the animals—the horses and ponies, the three dogs, two cats and of course the two pigs—it wasn't quite the same. Things were very quiet because everyone missed the human. The dogs moped about in the garden and didn't even venture over to see the pigs. The horses and ponies continued to eat the grass in their fields; but all around something was missing, and even Plumpkin and Penelope felt it and were behaving. Can you believe it? Those two mischievous pigs were actually doing as they were told. Well, there was no fun or excitement in their lives if they couldn't tease the human and the dogs, and these two new humans just weren't the same; they didn't know their little games and funny ways, so there wasn't any fun in being naughty. Or was there?

There was something odd about having to behave herself that Plumpkin couldn't quite get her head around. She needed her thinking time, that time of day when she could sort of snooze without sleeping and imagine all kinds of things, like what she could do next to cause a stir or what new place was just begging her to explore it. So, for a few days at least, those two naughty pigs actually did as they were told. Unfortunately there wasn't any fun or excitement, or need to squeal in delight, if they couldn't tease the dogs or the human, so Plumpkin decided after much deliberation that the new humans would just have to do.

"Thank goodness she's only gone for a week. All this lying around doing nothing isn't good for our figures," Plumpkin said to Penelope as they lay wallowing in their mud bath.

"What do you mean, not good for our figures?" Penelope asked.

"Well," Plumpkin offered, "here we are, eating all this food and not running any of it off. I can feel my waistline expanding by the day. Maybe she's fattening us up for market?"

"Are we going off to market?" Penelope asked with a quiver in her voice. She hadn't thought about going somewhere else; she thought this was her home for the rest of her life.

"I don't know!" Plumpkin yelled at her sister, as if something had just touched a nerve. The truth was, though, that she was big enough to go off to market, as she was nearly twice the size of Penelope and she knew it. She'd heard from a very reliable source (the sheep next door) that some farmers only reared animals to feed to humans. That was a fact.

At this stage Plumpkin and Penelope didn't know what they were being kept for, but I doubt it would have made much difference to Plumpkin either way; try as she might, she couldn't be good, not for long. Seven days of behaving nicely and not escaping was definitely too much to expect, and as you can probably guess, that certainly proved to be true in Plumpkin's case because she was bored and needed something new and exciting to do.

"What did you say about your waistline expanding? You don't have a waistline," Penelope muttered through a mouthful of mud. She just wanted to see the reaction it caused for her sister, who seemed a little distant, seemingly lost in her own thoughts. *I hope she's not thinking of doing something naughty*, she suddenly thought as she realised the days of peace and quiet might be coming to an end. "Oh, if only they could last a little longer. I was just getting used to doing nothing," she sighed, pushing her snout deeper into the soft, gooey mud.

"Did you say something?" Plumpkin asked, looking at her sister with mud dripping off the end of her snout.

"No, but if I had a camera I could take the funniest picture of you looking so beautiful," Penelope snickered, turning herself around to get the other side of her body just as muddy. What a delightful sight the two of them made, lying side by side in their bath of liquid mud, smiling as if they were in piggy heaven.

Plumpkin just couldn't stop her mind from thinking as she lay basking in the warm pool of mud. It was so hard not to plan a new game to play, especially as there were these new humans in the house who had never had the delightful experience of two adorable, naughty little—well, now not-so-little—pigs paying them a visit.

"Shall we go and visit the new humans?" Plumpkin asked, looking sideways at her sister in the hope that she would say yes. "It would be exciting, and I'm so bored," she sighed—one of those long, drawn-out ones to get her sister's sympathy.

"We promised the human we would be good girls and stay in our run," Penelope replied with just a hint of a smile on her face. She liked this new game of teasing her sister. It sort of made her feel grown up and for a change, in charge. Normally it was Plumpkin issuing the orders with Penelope obediently following on behind.

"We did no such thing. I never promised to be good," Plumpkin said as she stamped her trotter down into the soft earth at the edge of their mud bath, causing a splash. "We could just be very friendly, wander over very calmly and say hello, couldn't we?"

"What do you know about behaving like a good girl? Have you ever taken a leisurely walk? Do you know what a gentle stroll across the field is? No to all three! You don't even know how to," Penelope laughed, sitting back down in soft, liquid mud and making an even bigger splash. She was now very determined to make this discussion go on for quite a while because she had a feeling that it would be a long time before her sister would even consider listening to her again, so she was going to enjoy every delicious moment of it.

"I can be good—it's just that I'd rather be out there exploring," Plumpkin said, pointing her trotter towards the big field—and, of course, it just happened to point in the direction of the house too. She went on and on, trying her hardest and using all of her skills to break her sister down so that she would give in to her request. "Pretty please. Come on, sis, you know it'll be fun. Just say yes and let's get on with the adventure."

By the time Penelope finally gave in to her sister's demands it was late afternoon. The day had been so pleasantly warm that she thought a nice stroll across the field would be the perfect way to end such a lovely day. For once she had been able to tease her big sister, and she had enjoyed every delectable moment of it, so now she was quite happy to concede to Plumpkin's pleas of paying the new humans a visit.

"Okay, I give in. Let's pay them a courtesy call. Be gentle, though," Penelope spluttered, trying to catch her breath in order to shout out after Plumpkin, who had already disappeared under their secret escape route and was gone.

It is only by chance that I am able to tell you of this saga. On this particular day, I was minding my own business when out of the corner of my eye I caught a glimpse of something racing across the field. As I turned to get a better look, I saw Plumpkin charging as fast as her trotters could carry her towards the gate that led into the garden; she was obviously on a mission. I closed my eyes because I thought she would never stop in time to avoid hitting the gate, and when I didn't hear a crash or splintering of wood, I opened my eyes to see her flying over the gate like a show jumper. Right then and there, I thought to myself that there was going to be trouble as she landed on the other side and began running towards those poor young women, who were in for a shock when they realised what had just landed in the garden. Up until that moment they had been relaxing, sunbathing in the warm sunshine, but on seeing Plumpkin, coming towards them with her ears flapping, they started screaming and began to run towards the house. But then they stopped and did this funny jig, hopping up and down, going round in circles, holding on to one another and screaming. Well, I had to stick my claws into the bark of the branch I was sitting on; otherwise I would have fallen off from laughing so much. I knew Plumpkin didn't mean them any harm. I guess it was her way of saying hello, but the looks on their faces told a different story. Of course, the more they jiggled about and screamed, the more enthusiastic Plumpkin became in trying to make friends with them. I knew, and you probably know by now, that all she was seeking was a reward of food, but I guess for those two poor young women that wasn't their first thought. I watched with bated breath as they began to hop their way towards the house and safety, still gripping one another. I even heard Plumpkin call out to her sister to come and join the party, but Penelope, being the sensible one, declined.

"No thanks. I think one pig is enough for them for one day. Don't upset them anymore. Please come back," Penelope pleaded with her

sister again, but of course to no avail. Plumpkin was having too much fun to stop.

They eventually made it safely back to the house and quickly disappeared through the kitchen door, which slammed shut behind them, leaving you-know-who looking at them through the glass, licking her lips at the thought of what would soon be coming—food.

"What shall we do?" they both said in unison, looking to each other for help, still shaking from the shock of their surprise guest, who was still standing at the kitchen door and smiling at them through the glass panel. "We have to do something. We can't leave her out there. One of us has to be brave," the fair-haired one said, speaking with a little more composure and beginning to take charge of the situation.

"You do it. You're much braver than I am," the dark-haired one said, pushing her friend forward. "I'm afraid of pigs. They could eat us."

"Don't be silly—she's not big enough," her friend replied, beginning to laugh now at their situation. Here they both were, shaking like leaves on a tree because a pig had jumped into the garden and chased after them as they ran for safety.

"Send the dogs out. They can deal with her. I'm really scared. How safe is that door? Can she break it down? What shall we do?" the dark-haired one asked her friend, trembling and gripping her so hard that her knuckles turned white.

Of course, the dogs knew that they were of no use at all. Even though she was taller and younger than Ellie, Gem knew her limitations, and Ellie somehow knew that centuries ago they had hunted big boars and bears in the forests and woodlands, so she knew what this pig was capable of. This was why she would have preferred to stay safe indoors. As far as Gem was concerned, her most important job in life was to protect her human, whom she adored and followed around like a shadow. Now she was being asked to do her job and protect these shaking, trembling young women from this pig who would not do anything she was told and who, for all intents and purposes, was fearless. "Anna, we've got to do something. Any ideas?" Gem asked, turning to her best friend for inspiration.

Meanwhile, back to the frightened young women . . .

"What instructions were we given if the pigs escaped?" the fair-haired one asked her trembling friend, who was standing frozen in place, not daring to take her eyes off the door and the pig outside, just in case . . .

"How do I know? Look at the notes—they're there on the kitchen table, pages of them," the dark-haired one said, pointing backwards, not wanting to lose her focus. As much as she wanted to look away, she couldn't help herself—she had to keep watching that pig. The pig wasn't moving; she was just staring back at her. Somehow this made her feel safe.

Of course, the human had left lots of feeding instructions and what to do in case of emergencies. Written in big bold letters on the page were very simple instructions: "*IF THE PIGS ESCAPE, DON'T PANIC. THEY WON'T EAT YOU. THEY WILL FOLLOW YOU BACK TO THEIR PEN LIKE REALLY GOOD GIRLS IF YOU OFFER THEM FOOD. ANY FOOD WILL DO.*"

"See? It's simple," the fair-haired one said after reading the instructions. "We only have to offer her some food and she'll go home. That's probably what she's waiting for right now. Shall we try it?"

"There's just one tiny problem with your plan—their food is outside" the dark-haired one stuttered, thinking that any minute now the pig waiting outside would break down the door in her quest to be fed. However, we both know that Plumpkin was far too well-mannered to do that. She knew that if she stood there long enough, food would eventually come.

"Get the dogs. They'll chase her away," the dark-haired one shouted again as she ran through the house looking for the dogs, who by now had decided the best thing they could do was hide themselves away—pretending, of course, to be discussing a plan. Their past experiences with Plumpkin told them that once her mind was made up, nothing would stop her. Fortunately for them, help was just a moment away.

"Don't worry. I'll get her back in her pen. There's plenty of food in the kitchen to whet her appetite," came a voice from beyond as the fair-haired human rummaged through the cupboards. "There are plenty of biscuits and cakes that should make a good peace offering," she called loudly as she began opening the packets.

"You're so brave. Thank you," her friend called from the lounge, where she was now hiding with the dogs.

"Well, someone has to take charge and it's obvious you're no good. Why did you accept this job if you're so frightened of pigs?"

"I thought I would be able to manage, and, anyway, they weren't supposed to jump the fence. She never said they could jump."

"That's true. I guess you don't see flying pigs every day," said the fair-haired one, smiling to herself as she began to see the funny side of the day's excitement. "I'm off now. Come and rescue me if I scream."

"Don't say such things—you'll scare me even more. I'll watch you from the window. I've got my phone ready just in case."

"Come on, treasure," the brave fair-haired human said to Plumpkin as she opened the kitchen door. "See what nice goodies I've got for you," she said, showing Plumpkin the plate full of biscuits and cake in the hope that she would follow the bait—which, of course, like the good girl she was, she did right up to the garden fence. Plumpkin waited very politely for the gate to be opened and then followed the plate of biscuits and cakes into the field, where she was joined by Penelope, who had been waiting there all that time, not daring or wanting to join in. Being such good girls and wanting to make the right impression, they ran all the way back to their pen and waited patiently for their reward of biscuits and cake to arrive.

“Well,” Plumpkin said between mouthfuls, “I think that was a most successful outing.”

“I doubt whether those two young women will be saying the same,” Penelope laughed, admitting it had been a very funny spectacle to watch those humans. They had been so entertaining with their singing and dancing.

“Do you think it’s time for a bath?” Penelope asked with a large grin on her face.

“Most definitely,” Plumpkin replied. “A perfect ending to a perfect day,” she sighed as her head disappeared beneath the muddy water.

Chapter Eleven
Oh No! Not You Again!

"They haven't let us out this morning," Plumpkin complained to her sister.

"I'm not surprised after what you did to them yesterday. You'll be lucky if you ever get to go out into the field again, let alone find your way into the garden," Penelope replied rather sternly to her sister, although why she bothered she didn't know. As she looked around, she realised Plumpkin was nowhere to be seen. She'd already vanished into thin air.

"In case you're looking for me, I'm over here," Plumpkin shouted from the other side of the fence.

"How'd you get over there?" Penelope asked, quite flummoxed at seeing her sister already misbehaving.

"I knew you'd forgotten our secret hole, the one we were keeping for emergencies. Well, today was an emergency, so I used it."

"You can't be serious. You're not going back into that garden?"

"I am. You can stay there if you like or you can join me, but I'm going to pay those nice young women another visit. After all, it's the least I can do. I want to thank them for the delicious cake and biscuits we had yesterday."

"You'll only get into more trouble. Couldn't you just stay in the field?" Penelope pleaded, suddenly beginning to feel very sorry for those two girls. Yesterday's ordeal had been enough for them to cope with. "I don't think those young women will appreciate another visit from you so quickly. We were lucky we even got our breakfast this morning."

Penelope was vainly hoping that Plumpkin might just see sense and stay in the field. It wasn't as if they didn't have enough things to root around for. Only the other week they had found a little hidden garden which, to their surprise and utter delight, was full of tasty morsels such as carrots and runner bean plants. After tasting them they decided that they didn't like the squash plants, as the leaves were a little too prickly, so they left them. The carrots—now, they didn't normally do carrots, but the green tops and tiny orange roots were just yummy. They almost melted in their mouths, and those tiny red flowers on the bean plants were very tasty, so they just had to be eaten too. They thought it best to dig over the garden just to make sure they'd left nothing behind, and in doing so, of course, they managed to trample the squash plants they'd left. But otherwise you'd never have known they'd been there.

"Are you coming or not?" Plumpkin shouted. "I can smell food. Come on."

Should she be good and resist the temptation of following her sister on yet another one of her escapades? She could just lie down in the soft brown earth and go back to sleep, but there was just one problem: the smell of food coming from the house was too much to resist. In fact, it was enough to make up her mind.

"Oh, all right," she sighed. "I'll come, but wait for me before you do anything you'll regret." She already knew it was pointless to say something so silly.

She ran across the field between the remnants of discarded toys they'd been given to keep them amused. There were buckets that they liked to toss around and pull apart as they played their favourite game, tug-of-war, and there were long lengths of yellow piping flung all over the field, with bits of hosepipe and chewed connectors left lying around. Plumpkin just loved pulling the connectors off and drinking the water directly from the hosepipe. There were balls too for when they played football. So, you see, it wasn't as if they didn't have enough things to keep them occupied. It was just . . . you've got it. Plumpkin liked the thrill of escaping and making plans to escape.

Even though the young women had tried their hardest to reinforce the gate by attaching things to it, like odd bits of wood and plenty of string, it still wasn't pig-proof. In fact they had probably made it easier for them to climb over it instead of try to jump it, as Plumpkin had done yesterday.

"The gate's easy. On the count of three we'll climb over it. Ready? One, two, three," Plumpkin squealed in delight as her trotters began to climb up the rails, her mind already racing ahead at the thought of more food. They'd only just had breakfast, but that didn't seem to stop her. "Over there by the kitchen! They're sitting outside eating food. I told you I could smell it. Come on," Plumpkin squealed with excitement as she landed on the other side, and then she was off like a cannonball, running as fast as she could, squealing and grunting, big ears flapping over her eyes. What a sight for sore eyes, especially for both of those poor young women, but she knew exactly where she was going and, as usual, nothing was going to stop her.

Of course, the young women who were sitting outside enjoying their breakfast had thought it was safe to do so because the pigs were locked away in their pen. The garden gate had been reinforced, so there was nothing to worry about, was there? Now they could pretend they too were on holiday, except that two very naughty, not-so-little piglets had decided to spoil it by paying them another visit.

On seeing the two pigs running towards them, they both jumped up and screamed, dropping their plates of yummy food onto the floor, just waiting for two snouts to come and vacuum it up. Now *that* was an unexpected bonus.

The dogs, who were lounging outside too, saw what was occurring and beat a hasty retreat so that they could watch from a safe distance. Whilst hidden from view, they were able to watch the whole scene, which of course they found highly amusing. If only they had a camera. The dark-haired woman screamed like a banshee as she ran into the house and slammed the door behind her. Her friend stood her ground, feeling a little braver after yesterday's encounter, and happened to glance over her shoulder in the dogs' direction for some support—only they were too busy laughing to be of any real help.

The kitchen door opened slowly and ever so slightly, just wide enough so that a bag of food could be passed through the gap by the shaking hand of the dark-haired one as she held on to it. Remembering the instructions that had been left in case of an emergency—that, should the pigs escape into the garden and do what they shouldn't do, food in any form would get them back into their pen. The fair-haired one reached for the bag and began to shake it in order to get their attention.

"Told you it would be easy," Plumpkin grunted to her sister as they began to follow the young woman back towards their pen, already licking their lips at the prospect of tucking into the reward for their morning workout.

The game continued, of course, as it always did, with additions being added to reinforce the security of the garden gate.

"Very good," Plumpkin offered as a form of compliment as she stood watching from afar. "Those two girls are trying very hard to keep us out. They've even tied an old garden seat to the gate. I guess they'll try anything to stop us from getting into the garden and disturbing their peace. Shall we go and test it out?" she snickered in a joking tone.

"You're wicked, Plumpkin. Those poor girls will probably never rest now, at least not until our human comes home, because of what you've done to them," Penelope said as she too gave a little snicker.

"Okay, you win. We'll leave them alone now. We've had our excitement for the day, but you have to admit that it's been fun," Plumpkin said as she walked away from the fence, wiggling her curly tail and swishing it from side to side, feeling very smug and wearing a smile that went from ear to ear. Now, was that because she was thinking of something else to do to tease those poor young women, or was she content to enjoy soaking herself in a muddy bath? I'll leave you to decide.

Chapter Twelve
The Return

With the holiday over, things quickly returned to normal. The dogs came back to life, running into the field and barking their greetings once again to herald the arrival of food.

"Oh goody, I'm glad she is back. Yippee!" squealed Plumpkin with delight, licking her lips at the thought of more food, which of course was always a welcome treat. "We can start planning again now that she's back."

"Whoa there! Planning for what?" Penelope asked, gulping her food down, not sure that she really wanted to know the answer. Worry wrinkles were already beginning to appear on her face as she wondered what this planning might entail, but she already had a pretty good idea as to what it might be.

"Well, first off, we have to find a new way into the magical garden," Plumpkin hurriedly replied, trying to eat her breakfast as fast as she could. After all, there were things to do and she was eager to get started.

"Magical garden! What magical garden?" Penelope choked as one of the pig nuts got stuck in her throat.

"That's what I'm calling it from now on, because every time we go into the garden, something magical happens."

"Like what?"

"Food! Isn't that magical enough?" Plumpkin grinned in a funny sort of way, almost as if she were already there feasting on the treasure trove of delights this magical garden had to offer.

"Okay, so what's the new plan?" Penelope sighed, already resigning herself to being part of the double act and following her sister once more as they set out on their adventures into this magical garden. The past week, apart from the last two days, had been quite delightful as she'd lain about sunning herself, sleeping when she wanted to, soaking herself in the mud bath and indulging herself in all ways. When she felt the need, she dug into the soil using her strong snout, rooting around for tasty roots and shoots to nibble on, but most of all it was heaven just to be resting instead of escaping. If only it could have lasted a little longer. Never mind—there was always tomorrow, only she had a funny feeling that the new tomorrows were going to be anything but restful.

"Come on, sis, she's letting us out. That's got to be a good sign. Let's go," Plumpkin called out as her wiggly tail disappeared through the gate. "No time to waste—come on."

Dutifully, Penelope followed, although she chose to walk rather than run; after all, she knew exactly where her sister was heading and couldn't quite muster up the same enthusiasm.

"We'll check the fence first."

"Didn't we do that yesterday and the day before that, and the day before that too?"

"Yes, yes, I know we did, but she may have done something while we slept. See! Told you so," squealed Plumpkin as she came to an abrupt stop at the garden gate. Something new had been added to make it even higher, obviously in an attempt to stop her from climbing over it again. "She must have read my mind. I was planning on it being the same as yesterday so that we could have easily climbed over it. Now I'll have to think of something else," Plumpkin said as she scrunched up her snout in an attempt to think of a new plan.

"It must have been pretty obvious to her too," Penelope replied with just a hint of sarcasm in her voice. She was hoping that they could now concentrate on eating the grass in the field instead of searching for a new hole. "I'll leave you to search. Let me know when you find something." With that, Penelope walked away and left her sister to ponder. *There are more interesting things to find on the ground*, she thought as her large snout got to work sniffing out tasty shoots and roots to eat rather than finding new holes to crawl through.

As hard as she looked, Plumpkin couldn't find what she was looking for. There were no gaps big enough for them to squeeze through. That's the problem when you keep growing: what once appeared big or small suddenly doesn't seem quite the same, as the big is now small and the small—well, it's not even worth looking at, especially as these girls were now piling on the pounds.

"Come and eat," Penelope shouted with big juicy nettles hanging out of her mouth. "She'll have filled in all the gaps because those young women will have told her how naughty you were while she was away. We'll look again tomorrow."

Reluctantly, Plumpkin went to join her sister, and it was while she was munching on some fallen oak leaves that she caught sight of something out of the corner of her eye. This in itself was a miracle because her large ears flopped over her eyes, making her very nearsighted, except of course when she needed to see, like now. Over by the big gate, the one that all the ponies had walked through when they left the field to go across the road, she saw a hole. Excitedly she called out to her sister, "Look over there by the big field gate. What do you see?"

"What? Where?"

"Over there by the big gate," she pointed with her trotter.

"I can't see that far away, and neither can you."

"Come on, let's have a look," she said as she took off, running as fast as her little legs would carry her. She was sure that she'd spotted a new hole, and it couldn't possibly wait until tomorrow to be investigated. There was a hole, but was it big enough for her to scramble through?

"That's not big enough," Penelope said, even though she knew that Plumpkin would ignore her advice. "You can just about squeeze your head into it, but the rest of you will get stuck. Please don't try it. There's no way that hole is big enough, and I won't be able to pull you back out," she pleaded, trying to persuade her sister not to put her head into it.

Well, she might just as well have kept her breath in her body; no sooner had she spoken than Plumpkin disappeared through the hole. Now she was standing on the other side of the hedge with a great big smile on her face. As Plumpkin said those inviting words, "Come on, sis," Penelope knew that on this occasion she had to follow. It wasn't as tight a fit as she thought it would be, so she wriggled her body through and was soon standing next to her sister in the garden, the magical garden. This time, though, they were standing by another gate at the far end of the garden, one they hadn't noticed before that was quite a distance from Plumpkin's favourite place, the kitchen. Could this new gate lead them to new adventures?

Just as they were about to push the gate open in order to check out what was on the other side of it, the little black dog called Anna gave their game away as she started barking, which of course bought the human out to investigate what all the noise was about.

"Good girl, Anna," she said, patting her on the head before disappearing into the kitchen to get—yes, you've got it—food for those two naughty runaway pigs. Would she never learn?

"Come on, sis, we might as well give ourselves up and get our reward," Plumpkin offered as she began walking towards the house. The human stood watching as they approached. Without saying a word they obediently followed her back to their pen, but the look on Plumpkin's face was a picture. If it was anything to go by, then there was definitely another adventure in the offering.

Chapter Thirteen
New Adventures

Now, you don't think Plumpkin would give up that easily, do you? Not without some form of a plan hatching in her head. Well, of course, you're absolutely right. As far as those two naughty pigs were concerned, this new gate, which had until now been missed by Plumpkin's roving eyes and thorough investigations, now offered the promise of exciting new adventures to come.

The plan that she been formulating all night was not to give the game away too soon. They had to keep their new discovery a secret, as she didn't want the dogs to spot them as they had yesterday; undoubtedly they'd give the game away again, of that she was sure. No, they would have to be very vigilant when it came to wriggling through the hole and then turning a sharp right through the gate and out into the big wide world.

"Penelope, you go and saunter along the fence and see if anyone is about. Keep a sharp lookout for the dogs," Plumpkin ordered in her usual authoritative way.

"Aye, aye, Captain," Penelope smiled, tittering to herself. She just loved her sister and would do anything for her, and I suppose you could say that she led a very interesting and exciting life thanks to her sister and her escapades, although she occasionally yearned for a little peace and quiet. Having examined the garden as best she could with her limited eyesight (due to the very large ears that covered most of her little eyes), she decided that no one was about and was pretty sure she would have heard them if they'd been in the garden, even if she couldn't see them. "All clear, Captain," she called out to Plumpkin, who, unable to contain herself, was just about to wriggle through the hole. So much for her plan to be discreet.

"Come on then, what are we waiting for? Quick, before anyone sees us," Plumpkin, desperate to be off, said as her bottom disappeared through the hole. "Come on, sis," she said excitedly. "There is a whole new world out there beyond the gate just waiting for us to explore it."

"I'm on my way. Calm down. I told you no one is about, so what's the rush?"

"I want to see what's out there," Plumpkin said, beside herself with delight. She did a little wriggly dance in an attempt to curb her excitement. I think you could safely say that Plumpkin was going out of that gate and nothing was going to stop her.

With no effort at all, just a little push from Plumpkin's snout, the gate opened to reveal a whole new world. There was a road which they had only ever seen from the other side of the big gate. As they stood on the side of the road, it all looked so different, and they could see the stables and big concrete yard where Charlie Buttons, Tsar and the Shetlands lived with the other horses they had not yet met.

Plumpkin just couldn't contain herself. Squealing with excitement, she said, "This is such fun. Where shall we go first?"

"We could stay here," Penelope offered hopefully, not really wanting to go any farther. It all looked a bit too scary for her—too many choices and too much open space. She didn't feel safe. "Look, here's a nice wide verge with plenty of long grass. We could stay and eat," she said, trying to persuade Plumpkin not to go off wandering, but of course it fell on deaf ears.

"No! Come on, we've got to explore this road. Let's see where it goes to."

"To market!" Penelope cried out desperately, not wanting to go, but as usual Plumpkin was off running up the road—which, of course, meant that she had to follow. What else could she do? Someone had to keep an eye on such a wayward pig.

Fortunately a friendly neighbour spotted these two orange and black spotted pigs running up the road. Knowing that they shouldn't be there, she parked her car in the middle of the road to prevent any other cars from going up it whilst she went to find their owner, who was completely unaware of what these two naughty pigs had done.

A car parked in the middle of the road wasn't going to stop Plumpkin, not with all this new stuff to explore, so with her snout to the ground she was off. This was so exciting. There was so much to see and smell—

not that she could see that much, but the smells were wonderful.

Fortunately for them, another nice human had spotted them from the other direction, and she too had placed her car across the road to stop any other motorists from driving down the lane. As the pigs began to approach her, she began waving her arms in the hope that it would prevent them from going any farther, as just ahead was a very busy road with lots of cars, vans, tractors and big trucks driving really fast. Had they reached that busy road, they could have caused an accident, so this very nice lady was trying her hardest to stop them, and anybody else, from getting hurt.

Did the pigs understand her concerns, maybe? On seeing her waving her arms, they turned around just as help arrived in the form of their human running up the road, calling their names between laboured breaths and rattling something in a bucket. Yes, you've guessed it—food. Their reward again for escaping was more food. Was this human ever going to learn? These two pigs had her wrapped around their little trotters and were now laughing all the way home. Of course, as usual they showed her how good they were as they obediently walked behind, following the bucket that contained their reward. To any onlookers, and there were now a few, it looked as if they were very well-trained pigs. As usual, once they were safely ensconced in their enclosure, they received their reward of pig nuts. Yummy, and what an exciting day they'd had. There was nothing the human could say to them to make them understand the dangers of walking on the road, especially as they had no road sense. She was just relieved that no one had come to any harm.

Her main concern and worry was that they had a found a new way out of the garden and onto the road and that they would do it again—of that she was pretty certain based on their past record. So it was time to look at the fencing again and the hedgerows too, but as hard as she looked she couldn't find the tiny hole that had expanded enough for them to squeeze through. Even the dogs couldn't help her, although they tried their best. Was it going to be a case of wait and see, or would Plumpkin give in and stay in her field and make both the human and her sister happy?

Well, I guess in the language of those two naughty pigs, there was always tomorrow, and with those two, who knew what it would bring?

Chapter Fourteen
The Day of Five Escapes

Unsurprisingly, they didn't wait too long before venturing out onto the road again because, as you know, once Plumpkin found somewhere to squeeze her body through or over, she wasn't fussy; she would repeat the process again and again until it stopped. The hole they had recently discovered had not yet been found, so as far as they were concerned, they were free to roam wherever they liked. Fortunately, on this particular morning help was at hand to prevent them from going too far up or down the road, as they were spotted going through the garden gate by a young person who was there to play with the horses.

She quickly ran to the house, sounding the alarm that the pigs had escaped.

The human ran to the rescue, followed by the dogs and some other helpful souls who just happened to be visiting. Heavily armed with the usual bribe of food, she enticed them back into their pen, and as could be predicted, they followed the food, showing off to the large audience that had collected around them what amiable and good girls they were—really! It could have been because there were so many hands present and ready to assist them back across the field that they decided to cooperate so readily. I should say, though, that from where I was lying along my usual observational branch, the mildly irritated look on Plumpkin's face said that she wasn't so pleased to have been put back into her pen so soon. I had no doubt that even at this early hour of the day (it wasn't even ten o'clock), the cogs in her mind were turning and she had some audacious plan that she wanted to put into action.

"Never mind, sis, there'll always be another time," Penelope said to Plumpkin by way of commiseration for her failed idea for adventure that hadn't quite happened the way she'd planned it. Not that it mattered much to Penelope—to be honest, she was quite relieved. Besides, they'd managed to get an extra ration of food for their efforts. "I think you've done an amazing job of training our human to perfection, the way she keeps bribing us with so much food," she said, trying to brighten her sister's mood as she pondered for a moment on all the lovely food the human kept bringing them.

"What? What are you on about? Can't you see I'm busy thinking? We can't stay penned up in here all day," Plumpkin complained to her sister, obviously irritated, marching up and down their enclosure, snorting and grunting. "Not when we've discovered something so exciting. We should be out there exploring."

"Well, what do you suggest we do then?" Penelope sighed, already seeing trouble with a capital T approaching. *Maybe this would be a good day to bury my head and pretend to be asleep*, she thought. "Can't we just stay here and rest? We've already had extra rations. Can't you be content with that for today?"

"No! We have to figure a way out of here. We have to do something. Think!"

"I can't. I'm too tired. Let me sleep on it. I promise, when I wake up I will have thought of something. Just let me be."

"Okay, I'll let you sleep for now, only we have to get out. I'm itching to see more of that outside world." With that, Plumpkin went off and found a really strong post that she leant against, and then she went to town scratching her bottom, her sides, her face and her neck. "Ah! That feels better already. I guess I might as well join you, as there's nothing else to do at the moment," she said, snuggling down next to her sister.

Soon they both were sleeping like babies, which for some would be good news, but as you know, these pigs did lots of thinking while they were asleep. Somewhere in their minds a plan was being hatched which would be put into action when they awoke. The poor human didn't know what was coming, nor did anyone else for that matter. I thought today would have been a good day to have a camera ready to take some action shots, but as you are probably aware, cats don't really have a need for such a device. But I could tell by the way my whiskers were twitching that this was going to be one of those days.

Believing that her two naughty charges were safe and secure back in their pen and content with the extra ration of food they'd had, the human went off across the fields to do some work with the horses. Believe it or not, just recently a lot of her time had been taken up with doing other things, like the ongoing fencing repairs and looking for holes

that had been created by two very naughty pigs. So today she'd decided that it was going to be a horsey day, as they too deserved some of her time and attention—not that they seemed to mind too much. As long as there was grass in the field for them to eat, they appeared content.

No sooner had she started when she saw a woman walking across the field towards her. As she got closer she recognised her as one of the neighbours. Yes, you guessed it—she'd come to tell her that she had found the pigs outside her cottage, which was just up the road from their field, but not to worry because she'd brought them back. She said they'd been such good girls; all she had to say to them was "home" and off they'd trotted, back the way they came. She'd left them unattended by the garden gate.

Of course, when they got to the gate they were nowhere to be seen. The house—well, the kitchen and garden—were checked just in case, but nothing. They'd disappeared again.

"It's okay. I've spotted them!" the nice lady shouted. "They're up the road again. I can see my husband—he's waving his arms at them. He's trying to stop them going any farther up the road. We've got a dinner party tonight. What fun I'll have telling them about your pigs. Quick, before they escape him!" And with that, she went running up the road, followed by—you guessed it—the human with a bucket of food.

They were very good, of course, little paragons of virtue as they showed off to these new humans just how well-mannered and well-behaved they were, by following their human all the way home. Not a squeak or a squeal came from them, as they were too busy thinking about what was in the bucket, their mouths watering at the very thought of yet another meal.

The human again left them safely in their pen while she went across the road to get the usual tools and materials she thought she would need to mend the fence, although she had no idea where they were escaping from. She really thought their large enclosure was pretty pig-proof. Well, before you could say "pretty pigs," they were off again, running across the field as fast as their little legs could carry them. They were definitely on a mission. Had something happened today to make them so mischievous, or was it just one of those days? I'll leave you to figure that one out.

"Oh no you don't!" she shouted at them as she spotted them heading towards the big field gate, still unaware that there was a hole in the hedge which they could squeeze and wriggle their bodies through. "Get back now!" she shouted, pointing her finger in the direction she wanted them to go.

"Best do as she's asking." Plumpkin slowed down.

Penelope winked at her. "We'll pretend to stay put till she's gone away, and then we'll make our escape again."

"Good thinking, sis. She'll never find our new way out, thanks to you."

After a thorough check of all the fences, there were no more rails to put up, or string to be tied to hold things together, or even any nails to be banged in, because try as she might, she just couldn't find the new hole they were escaping through. So there was no other choice: she would have to lie in the long grass and wait for them. She had a funny feeling that today, for whatever reason, they were too full of mischief not to try to escape again. The magnetism of the road appeared too much for them to resist. Watching with great interest from my perch on the branch of the large willow that overlooked the field and garden, I had the best view of all the goings-on, and at times I had to cling on with my claws because I was laughing so much. Even I couldn't begin to figure out how Plumpkin managed to be so naughty. Maybe it was something in the water. They were definitely on a roll. I couldn't have made up a story like this if I'd tried, and it certainly kept me entertained. I have to tell you that every one of their escapades was true. At times I felt really sorry for our human, as she looked after all of us so well that she didn't deserve the games they played on her. On the other hand, if they weren't so naughty, there wouldn't be all these wonderful tales to tell you, would there?

From the way the human walked back to the house to put the dogs away, I could tell she wasn't a very happy person. I guess she was worried that they might get hurt or, even worse, hurt someone else. I knew she couldn't have the dogs with her, as their wagging tails would give the game away by showing the pigs where she was hiding. The dogs wouldn't know that she wasn't there to play with them, but on a secret mission to find out how and where those naughty pigs were getting out. So, leaving the dogs in the house, she crept back into the field and waited. She didn't have to wait too long, as those naughty pigs just couldn't resist the urge to use their new escape route again.

I watched in disbelief as they both squeezed themselves through a gap between the hedgerow and the fence of the farmer's field next door. Then they climbed up a tree using the lower branches to help them gain the height they required in order to jump over the fence that was supposed to keep them in. As soon as their trotters touched the ground, they were off again and running across the field, straight towards their little hole and freedom. It took a few seconds to register, and then the human had to run as fast as she could. I knew that she knew exactly what was on their minds, as they were already trying to squeeze through the hole into the garden. And guess what? She'd gone and left the garden gate open. She only just managed to get to the gate before they did, and was trying her hardest to stop them from pushing past her, when I saw alarms go off in her head as she remembered something else, something equally important: the gates to the front drive were wide open. I think at that moment she had a very funny feeling as she realised that today being today, if they couldn't get out of the small garden gate, they would look for another escape route to get back out onto the road. What a to-do!

Fortunately, just when she needed some help, it came in the shape of a neighbour who just happened to be passing by in her car with the windows down because it was such a nice day. Perhaps it was the sunshine that had stirred these pigs into action; something certainly had.

"Stop!" she shouted. "I need your help. Please, would you close my front gates? The pigs have escaped and I can't leave this gate!"

"What?" the neighbour shouted back.

"I need you to close my front gates. The pigs have escaped!" she repeated.

I know you're wondering why she couldn't leave the garden gate to run and close the front gates herself. Well, you see, this particular gate didn't have any means of being fastened. There were no bolts or catches to keep it shut, and she knew that the bit of string that was there holding it shut wouldn't be strong enough to hold them in. So much for forward planning! It wasn't as if they hadn't warned her. After all, they'd already escaped through it—three times!

So what happened next? Well, the neighbour saved the day by managing to close the front gates in time. The girls gave up trying to get through the gate that the human was defending and decided instead to explore the garden in case the dogs had left anything out, like an old bone or dog chew, which they sometimes did. This gave the human time to go and get more tasty treats to tempt them back into their run.

"She'll have to offer us something really tasty this time," Plumpkin said, already licking her lips in anticipation of what was to come.

"Yummy!" Penelope squealed as they both tucked into the assortment of hastily collected bananas, biscuits and chocolates.

"Do you think we should have one more go?" Penelope asked, watching her big sister chomp away on a mashed-up banana. For a change, she'd really enjoyed escaping today. Perhaps it was the sunshine or the thought of even more food to come that prompted her to ask, and they hadn't even had their proper tea yet.

"I don't see why not. Come on, let's do it before she comes back."

Meanwhile, the human was filling a wheelbarrow with big planks of wood, wire, nails, a big hammer and some wooden stakes. She meant business this time and was determined to stop them once and for all.

This time, though, something was different when she entered the field and went towards their pen. There were no pigs inside the pen; they'd gone yet again. So where were they? Looking carefully around, the human saw no obvious signs at first and heard no rustling of leaves or snapping of branches—only silence. And then, from an area of the field that she'd never checked before, came two sorrowful little piggies that didn't look very well at all. In fact, they looked a funny shade of green. With their heads hung low, they slowly made their way towards her and, without any prompting, went straight into their pen.

"We don't want any tea tonight. We feel a bit sick. We forgot to tell you that we're not supposed to eat chocolate," Penelope murmured as she slowly walked past the human. All she wanted to do was go to bed.

For the first and perhaps the only time, they didn't end their exciting day with a mud bath or pleasant dreams; instead they curled themselves up on their straw beds and promised never to eat chocolate again.

Chapter Fifteen
Is She Never Satisfied?

You would think that by now the human would have got everything worked out—escape meant a reward of food, fences and gates needed to be fastened securely—but, I have to tell you, she still hadn't clocked on to what these naughty pigs were up to, as it appeared that nothing could deter them from trying to escape. Whilst sometimes it might take them more than a couple of days to work out a new escape route, invariably they succeeded and were, of course, always rewarded with more juicy, mouthwatering treats (but not chocolate), which encouraged them to escape even more.

On one occasion as they explored the garden yet again, they found the greenhouse. It didn't contain anything really exciting or interesting in the form of food, only tomato plants, which they found rather distasteful and spat out. The only trouble was that after having found their way in through the doorway, there wasn't enough room for both of them to turn around and go out of it. So guess what? Have you guessed correctly? Yep! They both went through the side, smashing the panes of glass as they went, unhurt and unshaken with not even a bristle on their backs damaged. They continued to run around the garden, searching for more things to eat or root up. Anything that the dogs might have left lying around would be of interest to them; an old bone or half-eaten dog chew would do nicely.

Anna the little black dog, who was a year younger than Gem, had lots of energy and was very fast on her feet. Once she worked out that the pigs weren't going to eat her, she decided that she quite liked it when they visited the garden because it meant that she could play with them. She liked running after them as if they were playing tag. Actually, they were really good at playing games. Well, both you and I know that they were taught to play games by Monty and Tilly, the little Shetlands who had shared their field with them when they were much smaller piglets. When it came to playing, Anna was very careful and respectful of them because she knew that they had lots of teeth in their very large mouths. She'd seen what they could do with one of her old bones, and although she knew that they were very friendly, sometimes they got a little too close for comfort. *It would have been nice*, she thought, *to have been able to keep them out of trouble, but trouble seems to follow them around*. Anyway, they kept growing and growing, and it seemed nothing could stop them from getting into mischief.

On another occasion they found some cans of beer outside the back door. This was on one of their early morning raids into the "magical" garden.

"Yummy!" Plumpkin squealed as the bubbles, created by her shaking the can as she bit into it, went up her nose. Emptying the amber liquid down her throat, she began to hiccup, which made her laugh. Penelope couldn't see what was so funny until she did the same thing, and then she too was hiccupping and laughing. They'd had so much fun, and believe it or not, they actually took themselves back to their pen without any prompting or reward of food. Suddenly they felt quite sleepy and in need of a lie-down. By the time the human awoke, all she found were the empty, pierced cans lying around the backyard with no pigs in sight, only the evidence of their having been there.

All those extra rations that they'd received as a reward for escaping had helped to pile on the pounds. They also began to find that their favourite holes through which they escaped were beginning to disappear, and that they now needed to find bigger and bigger holes which they could squeeze their now larger bodies through. Of course, these holes were very obvious to the human eye, so it became more and more difficult for them to escape and create mischief, although Plumpkin, never one to miss an opportunity, was always looking for something to enliven her day.

And so one day, much to her amusement, the human herself came up with a new venture for the girls when she thought they could be of some help in eating the roots of the bulrushes and reeds that had grown so profusely in the pond across the road. The pond had dried out during the long, hot days of the summer, and she thought that now would be a good time for the girls to have a root around and help tidy it up.

Would you think this was a good idea, knowing the sort of dastardly pigs they were? Perhaps you wouldn't attempt such a feat, especially knowing that the first thing you had to do was get them across the road. As far as the human was concerned, this wasn't a problem. She didn't think crossing the road would be such an obstacle, even though she knew how much the pigs liked to explore new places. Now, we know the road to them was just a new way to a different adventure, so with the help of two friends brought in specially for this occasion, they were sort of escorted across the road with the assistance of a rather large bucket of food, rattling away so as to keep them occupied. Otherwise, who knows what might have happened? I have to tell you that the first plan was to place a rope around their necks so that they could be led around like dogs on a lead, only this didn't quite work out as the human had hoped, probably because at that stage no food was offered. We all know how much Plumpkin liked her food and how obedient she was when it was put right in front of her, so when she saw the rope, she thought it was a new game to play and kept running off, squealing as she went. This was another one of those occasions when I wished I had a camera to capture the moment because, I can assure you, it was a curious and highly amusing spectacle. I can honestly say that the dogs were not much use when it came to making the pigs move; only food had the desired effect.

"What do you think she will want us to do today?" Penelope asked her sister as they were being coaxed into following a rather large bucket of food.

"I don't know, and I don't really care," Plumpkin replied. "I just want those strangers to stand still long enough so that I can get my head in the bucket. Why do they keep moving?"

"They're taking us somewhere. Do you think we're going to market?" asked Penelope with a rather worried look on her face.

"Don't be silly. We're not going to market. How would we get there?"

"Oh! I see what you mean. There'd be a trailer to take us, like the one we came in."

"Yes, and there isn't, so we're safe. She obviously has a plan—we just don't know what it is yet. I'll follow the food and you follow me. Don't worry, I have a feeling that we're going to have some fun."

Now Penelope was worried. Whenever her sister mentioned the word "fun," it usually meant trouble, and today was probably going to be no exception.

Obediently the girls followed the bucket of food across the road, through the farm buildings and out into the back field where the pond was. Someone had been very busy erecting an electric fence around the pond, presumably in the hope that it might just be sufficient to keep two pigs safely within its boundary.

"Wonder what that's for?" whispered Penelope to her sister, who was busy tucking into the nuts that had just been thrown onto the ground in a line for her to follow, leading across the fence and into the pond.

"What? Did you say something?" Plumpkin asked, looking up in time to see the fence and the ponies, who were busy grazing in the distance, completely unaware that two not-so-little pigs had just entered one of their fields.

"Look!" Penelope squealed. "There's Charlie Button and the Shetlands!" And with that she was off, running towards them and leaving her sister still eating. Fortunately for everyone, a wooden post and rail fence stopped her actually going into the field where the horses and ponies lived. She looked for a gap in the fence but couldn't find one, which was just as well because horses and pigs don't really mix, and although Charlie Buttons, Monty, Tiger Tom, Hettie, Roxy and Tilly were acquainted with them, the bigger horses weren't. We all remember how Tsar didn't find them to his liking.

Charlie Buttons was on his way over to the water trough when he saw a familiar shape running along the fence. *What's that?* he thought, squinting to get a better look. "Oh no, not those two!" he shouted out loud as he began to run towards the fence with his ears flat against his head as a warning to stay away. Of course, you and I know that these pigs didn't have the best eyesight in the world, and even if they did, they didn't speak horse, so they wouldn't know that ears pinned back against the head was a signal to beware.

"Hi, Charlie Buttons, it's me!" Penelope squealed, running along the fence to greet her old friend, thinking that because he was running towards her, he was pleased to see her too. It was only when she saw his head pointing towards her like a battering ram that she thought, *He doesn't seem that pleased to see me*. "Charlie, it's me," she repeated. "Don't look so angry. I thought you'd remember me."

"Remember you I do," Charlie replied, his ears at last standing upright as they should and his face a little softer and less angry now that he was talking to her. "The last time I saw you, you were only a little piglet. Now you're really big and a bit scary. The bigger horses will freak out if they see you. They're frightened of you as it is when they see you and your sister lying by the big gate sunbathing. They think you'll escape and eat them. You're not welcome or safe here, so please go home."

"But, Charlie, I thought you'd be pleased to see us again," Plumpkin said with a quiver in her voice and a tear in her eye, upset by Charlie's reaction.

"I'm sorry, Penelope. I didn't mean to upset you—please don't cry. It's just that I know if the others saw you, they would attack you because they would see you as a threat. There are too many of them, and I don't want to see either you or your sister hurt, so please go away."

"Okay, Charlie," she said, and she walked away with her head held a little lower than usual, back towards the pond where Plumpkin was still busy eating, turning the soft brown mud over with her nose, completely unaware that her sister had been talking to Charlie.

While Penelope had been trying to talk to Charlie, the human had been watching, carefully noting the reaction of Charlie towards Penelope, and was now a little concerned about whether she'd done the right thing by bringing them over. If they succeeded in clearing the pond out, then it would have been worthwhile. Just as a precaution, though, she switched the electric fence on as soon as Penelope joined her sister so that if they attempted to escape, it would give them a small shock. Well, that was the plan.

Having got bored very quickly rooting around in the soft silt of the pond, Plumpkin found those roots really weren't to her liking and thought that there must be something better in the field to eat. She looked up, and as she did so she finally espied Charlie, who was standing by the fence. Thinking that he was waiting for her to say hello, she began to run directly towards Charlie and the electric fence.

"No, Plumpkin, you can't," Penelope called after her, but it was too late. Plumpkin was heading straight for the fence and Charlie. Suddenly something struck her, which caused her to stop—but only momentarily, though, for she continued to run as fast as she could, pulling the electric fence behind her. The fence was no longer working, as it had disconnected from the battery when she ran through it. The ping of electricity appeared to have no effect upon her; it didn't even slow her down, as she was on a mission to see her old friend Charlie Buttons.

"Plumpkin, don't," Penelope called after her. "He doesn't want to say hello—he wants us to go away. Please, Plumpkin!" she squealed, closing her eyes because she didn't really want to look at what Charlie might do to her sister as she approached the fence. She heard the squeal and knew that Charlie had bitten her—probably the only thing that would have stopped her—but then something else happened.

Plumpkin's squeal had been so loud that the other horses heard it and were now running over to see what all the commotion was about. Oh dear! Too many hooves and teeth and angry faces were now looking over the fence at these two interlopers.

"Who and what are they?" Annie asked, standing back as far away as she could with her nostrils flared and eyes wide open, wanting to get a better look at them yet scared at the same time.

"They're the pigs from across the road!" Monty shouted, pleased to see them. "Wow, you've grown. You're nearly as tall as me now. What are you two doing here?" he shouted, trying to make himself heard above the noise that everyone was now making.

"The human brought us over to eat the weeds in the pond, but I guess by the looks on everyone's faces they're not too happy about us being here!" Plumpkin shouted back. "Do you think it might be a good idea if we left?" she asked Monty, just as Misty was stretching his neck out as far as he could with his mouth wide open, ready to bite her.

"I think now would be a good time to run!" Monty shouted at her. Obeying his instructions immediately, she sprinted away from the fence just as Misty brought his head down to land on her back. Fortunately she was gone before he had time to bite her, and instead the only taste of pig that he got was a few bristles from the end of her curly tail.

"Yuck!" he said as he spat the bristles out of his mouth and shook his head in disbelief.

"Phew, that was a narrow escape. Let's go home. It's not safe here," Plumpkin said to Penelope, who had watched the whole spectacle with her mouth open. There was nothing she could say or do except follow her sister, who was now making her own way through the farm buildings. Standing, waiting patiently for the humans to catch them up and take them back to the safety of their own field, she said as they approached, "I hope they never ask us to do something for them ever again. Pond weeds indeed—they didn't even taste nice. Somehow I don't think the human will be asking us to dig her pond again."

"I don't think she will either," Penelope said with a very large smile on her face. It had been a very interesting afternoon, one that neither of them would forget in a hurry.

Chapter Sixteen
Pigs Can Fly

"What is she looking at?" Plumpkin asked as she turned towards her sister. "Why is she standing in the middle of the field like that?"

"How do I know? I can't read her mind. I don't know what she's doing," Penelope replied, sounding a little annoyed. It was times like this when she wished that she could read the human's mind, and then she could give her sister the answer she wanted—which hopefully would then keep her quiet. They certainly didn't have any trouble making the human understand them. As it happened, their demands were quite simple:

a nice clean bed, fresh water, exercise and of course food. As they stood and watched their human, they could tell she was definitely up to something—but what?

The girls had been quite active since their trip across the road. Although they hadn't been successful in clearing the pond of its reeds due to the unforeseen circumstance, it had helped them in other ways; now when their tea was late in arriving, they took it upon themselves to wander over to the stables to remind the human that they needed to be fed. Well, she couldn't keep two hungry tummies waiting, could she? It was her own fault; she'd shown them where to go, so she only had herself to blame when they turned up demanding food. As usual, they were taken back to their field with the reward of food that they'd been after. There was still one tiny problem: she didn't know how or where they were getting out. It certainly wasn't through the fence; by now they were too big to fit through the rails, and any holes that did appear were now too obvious. Just in case, they got filled in with lots of bits and pieces, so they definitely had a secret way out and they were keeping it that way. Mind you, I could have told the dogs where to look, but why should I and spoil everyone's fun? I decided on this occasion that I would keep their secret a secret.

So, going back to the human standing midway across the field, I can't tell you why it hadn't happened before. I guess it was just one of those things. On this particular morning, as she was walking back across the field, she stopped and looked, exclaiming out loud so that we could all hear her, "You silly idiot, you've only gone and built them a playpen with ladders. No wonder they keep escaping—they're climbing up the fence!" Of course, this was exactly what they'd been doing since they'd become too big to squeeze themselves through it.

Without any delay she went off to buy new fencing, "I'll stop them once and for all," she said out loud to the dogs, who of course understood everything she said as they lay there watching her, smiling to themselves. Of course they knew what these naughty pigs had been up to, but now their adventures were definitely coming to an end.

This time she picked a fence that had lots of small upright posts wired together called palings. *There is no way that they can climb up this one*, she thought. Well, by now we all know that Plumpkin and Penelope just loved a challenge.

"What do you reckon then?" Plumpkin asked her sister as they lay sunning themselves right next to the newly erected fence.

"It looks very nice, doesn't it? You're not thinking of climbing over this one, are you? There's no way, Plumpkin. Don't you even think about it," Penelope coughed and laughed at the same time as she turned over. "You'll never do it."

"I'm working on a new plan right now. It may take a little while, but I'm sure we can succeed," Plumpkin offered as she too turned over, wanting to get an even tan on her rather large body. Closing her eyes, she began to dream, and in her dream she saw herself flying over the fence. *That's it*, she thought when she woke up. *That's the way over. Now all I have to do is find "the way."*

"I'm fed up. We need some excitement. All this lying around isn't good for our figures," Plumpkin said as they both lay by the big field gate that opened out onto the road. This had become their new favourite place to lie because from here they could see the horses and ponies across the road—not that they wanted to see the pigs. However, now that Plumpkin and Penelope knew that the other animals were frightened of them, they thought it was the best game ever, so they teased them by standing on their back legs and peering over the gate. I have to say that this was a very impressive sight, one that certainly caused the horses to stare in disbelief. Only these two could be cheeky enough to do it. I knew, though, that there was another reason they liked lying there: they had a good view into the garden, so they could watch the human and the dogs as they went about their daily business.

"I spy with my little eye something beginning with the letter V," Penelope whispered into her sister's ear.

"What did you say?" Plumpkin asked in a rather gruff voice. "You've gone and broken my thoughts. Now where was I?"

"She's got a visitor," Penelope whispered again as if teasing her sister.

"I heard you this time. Oooh! I think that this would be the perfect day to put my plan into action, and we can say hello at the same time," Plumpkin said excitedly as she sat up.

"What do you mean, say hello?" Penelope looked at her sister and shook her head in disbelief. "We can't just pop into the garden uninvited, and anyhow, excuse me for asking, but just how do you propose we get into the garden?"

"I have a plan. I've been working on it for days now. Every day I've been digging the dirt away from the bottom of the fence to loosen it.

See?" she said as she hooked her trotter under the fence. "I've been pulling at it so that now I can pull it out at an angle."

"I wondered what you'd been doing, but why does it have to be at an angle?" Penelope asked, a little bewildered, thinking that perhaps the sun had got to her sister and was making her a little confused.

"My plan is this," Plumpkin said in a matter-of-fact way, as if she'd got it all worked out. "If we can pull the fence out far enough, we'll then have a ramp to run up, and then we'll just fly over the fence and land in the garden."

"Run up and fly? You must be joking," Penelope said, trying her hardest not to giggle.

"No! I'm serious. I've worked it all out. We just need to run up the ramp as fast as we can."

"Have you seen how narrow those palings are and how big our trotters are in comparison?" Penelope asked, looking directly at her sister only to see that she was very serious about this proposed plan.

"Yes! Yes, I know, but it will work—trust me. Run fast and the rest of us will follow."

"What do you mean the rest of us will follow?"

"Well, once we're airborne the weight of our bodies will help us to land."

"Airborne! You mean flying?"

"Yes, flying! We'll be flying through the air. That's how we'll get over the fence, and when we're in the garden we can go and say hello."

"Never! Pigs fly never. Who's ever heard of such a thing? Pigs don't fly. You won't get me flying." Penelope shrugged her shoulders and began to walk away, thinking that her sister really had gone mad and lost the plot.

"Come on, sis, don't be a spoilsport. It has to be worth a go. At least try. Please. Think of all the nice food waiting for us, and the nice surprise her guest will have when we run over to say hello."

"The shock, you mean. Have you forgotten how those other girls reacted when they saw you? She may not even like us."

"Don't be silly. Everyone likes us! We're so cute and adorable," Plumpkin snickered.

"I can think of plenty of horses who don't think that we're so cute and adorable," Penelope offered as a way of bringing her sister back down to earth.

"Oh, them! They don't count. They love us really—they just don't know it yet. We'll grow on them, just you wait and see. Come on, stop moaning and help me pull the fence out before it's too late."

"Okay, but on one condition."

"What's that?"

"I get the food first."

"Deal. Come on," Plumpkin squealed in delight. She knew her sister couldn't resist such an opportunity; she'd been waiting days for the right moment to arrive and now it was here, a chance to put her theory to the test. *Just perfect*, she thought as she positioned the fence with the help of her sister, to just the right angle for a perfect takeoff. "Now remember, run as fast as you can. Don't worry about where your feet go—just keep running and then fly. I'll go first. Watch me."

Positioning herself as far back in the field as she could, Plumpkin began to run as fast as her legs would carry her. Once she hit the wooden fence she ran up it and then flew through the air, shouting and squealing "Yippeeeeee!" at the top of her voice, followed immediately and successfully by Penelope.

"Did you see that?" the visitor said, looking quite startled at what she'd just seen. She jumped to her feet and began to walk towards her friend. "I would never have believed it if I hadn't seen it with my own eyes. Pigs flying through the air—how did they do that? Remarkable, they're unbelievable," she said, holding on to her friend's arm, not quite sure what to do next.

"I know," her friend replied with a note of exasperation in her voice. "I don't know what I'm going to do with them. They're so naughty," she said, smiling. No matter how much she tried, she just couldn't get cross with them, especially now that they'd just flown into her garden and were running over to see her with their tails wagging as if they were pleased to see her. Flying pigs. Whatever next?

Chapter Seventeen
The Last Adventure

What can I say? Would these two naughty pigs ever learn to behave themselves? Did the human really want them to behave? After all, they did keep her on her toes, and they provided us all with lots of stories to tell about their exploits and adventures, even if it appeared that they had the upper hand.

Somehow or other, they had established a daily ritual of visiting the garden to see if the dogs had left anything out for them to find in the form of a tasty bone or chew, which did very nicely as a little snack. Then they took themselves back into their field.

Everyone had got used to these visits. The dogs accepted this routine by lying there, seemingly unperturbed. They even allowed them to come close enough to sniff them. I'm not sure whether the dogs allowed this close contact because they knew the pigs weren't going to hurt them or because they were too scared to move. Or were they just resigned to the fact that they weren't going away, so they just had to let them do what they had to do? I'll leave you to decide, as I've given up trying to make any sense of it. I think, personally, based on my very astute observations that they had managed to train everyone beautifully to perfection, which allowed them to do just as they pleased.

They just loved lying by the big gate, as it amused them so much knowing that they were teasing the horses across the road, especially when they stood on their back legs using the gate as a support while they looked directly across at them, knowing it would frighten them. It didn't matter how many times they did this; the result was always the same. The horses would huff and puff, snort and cough, their ears pricked, and then they'd all run off, as if some imaginary beast was chasing after them while those naughty girls rolled around on the gravel, holding their sides and laughing.

"Will they ever learn?" Plumpkin chortled as she composed herself.

"You'd think by now that they would have worked it out that we can't actually get to them."

"They're just being silly. Maybe they know it's a game and they're just playing along with us," Penelope snickered, finding it all so amusing. It did help to pass the day.

Try as they might, they just couldn't help themselves; they had to keep looking and checking the fences and hedges. Well, you never know—a hole might suddenly appear, and then they could have a new adventure.

Autumn had arrived, which brought with it many changes. The leaves on the trees and hedgerows were fast disappearing, falling to the ground and leaving bare branches, and guess what? Holes started appearing, small ones at first, and then bigger ones began to emerge.

"Look here! Never seen that one before," Plumpkin shouted to her sister as she prodded the hedge with her very strong and powerful snout, which could now push its way through anything. "Look! It's loose, and there's a really big gap behind it. Quick, follow me." And with that, she was gone.

"Wait for me," Penelope called out after her, running over to where her sister had been foraging.

"There, right in front of you. Just push and you'll be through."

"Where are we?" Penelope asked, looking around as she found herself on the other side of the hedge, in a place they'd never seen before.

"I don't know. Look, there's another hole. Come on, we'll explore and find out," Plumpkin said, already making her way towards another rather large hole that led them directly into a very large field, which had been planted with winter wheat that was already beginning to shoot. "This is fun!" shouted Plumpkin as she began to munch on the very nice, tasty green shoots.

As far as the human and the dogs were concerned, it was a quiet, relaxing Sunday. They thought the pigs were just being very good, completely unaware that the two larger-than-life characters were missing. It was not until teatime came that it became apparent that they'd gone on a walkabout. Then the panic set in.

Calling out their names as loudly as she could revealed nothing. Checking the roads revealed nothing. Walking across the road and the fields out the back revealed nothing. The pigs were nowhere to be seen. No matter how much rattling of the bucket was done, it didn't summon them. It was quiet, too quiet. Maybe someone had kidnapped them, led them away without anyone noticing.

Meanwhile, two large pigs were quite content and far too busy enjoying themselves in this new wonderland, completely unaware of the anguish their absence was causing. It wasn't until it began to get dark that they suddenly realised it was time for bed. Normally they were very good when it came to bedtime, as they liked to be tucked up in bed just before sunset and fast asleep before it got dark.

"Oops! I think we may have stayed out too long. Quick, run!" Penelope shouted to her sister, who was still busy rooting around in the soft soil.

"What? Oops, it's late," Plumpkin said, suddenly realising that the sun had already set and the light was beginning to fade. She began to run after her sister, who was already halfway across the field.

From a distance the human who'd continued to search and call out to them suddenly spotted two rather large bodies with flapping ears running across the field towards her.

"At last they've got the sense to come home," she sighed with relief, happy to see their smiling faces getting closer and closer.

Now the dogs could stop fretting too, as they had been busy searching here, there and everywhere for those wayward pigs. I had been on my usual perch, observing all the comings and goings with a large grin on my face. I liked it when the pigs were naughty.

"Where have you been, you naughty girls? I was so worried about you. I thought someone had taken you away and all the time you were in the field next door. The farmer will be really cross if he ever finds out what you've been up to in his field. What am I going to do with you two?" she sighed, leading them back across the field to put them away for the night. That was the new compromise. They now had the full run of the fields during the day and they got locked in their run at night, and each morning they would wait patiently to be let out.

Only when they awoke the next morning, something was different; the gate which was normally locked was open, but the gate which was normally open was now closed.

"Do you think we overstepped the mark yesterday?" Plumpkin asked as she turned to look at her sister, who looked just as bewildered as she was.

"I think we may just have blotted our perfect copy book, and now we're locked in," Penelope answered. Although puzzled and perplexed, she had a funny feeling that the days of their adventures had finally come to an end. Still, there was one consolation: they could now concentrate on what pigs do best, dig.

It is only fair that I tell you that those two rather naughty and certainly mischievous pigs had really overstepped the mark by going into the field next door. It was one thing to escape and go walk about, but to dig and root on someone else's property was not permitted. It meant that the human had only one course of action left to take, and that was to lock them in. She gave them a whole field to themselves so that they could dig to their hearts' content, rooting around as pigs do with their very powerful snouts. And so it came to pass that Plumpkin and Penelope found themselves with so much digging to do that somehow escaping, exploring and adventures took second place. From the moment they got up in the morning to when they retired to bed at night, with of course lots of little snooze times in between, they were so busy doing their housework (that is, digging) that there was no time left to scheme and plan. Eventually the field was full of furrows, mounds and big holes the likes of which we had certainly never seen before. I'm sure to Plumpkin and Penelope it was a masterpiece, a sculpted work of art that they had lovingly laboured over. It certainly gave a chuckle to the many visitors that came to view it.

They even had a new home, the "palace," specially built for them on stilts so that they didn't have to sleep on the damp earth. (Apparently the human had read somewhere that it was much nicer for them.) So, as the story goes, they lived happily ever after.

There is just one final thing that I should tell you which you may or may not find amusing. It took several weeks for the human to realise that there was something missing in her life. Can you guess what that was? Well, I shall tell you. Her world was now peaceful and silent without the grunts and squeals that usually came from the pigs with their demands for food, for now they were quite content and silent to receive their two meals a day. So everyone lived happily ever after.

Review Requested:
If you loved this book, would you please provide a review at Amazon.com?
Thank You

Lightning Source UK Ltd.
Milton Keynes UK
UKOW07f1554050815

256421UK00004B/30/P